# The Royal Diaries

# Nzingha

## Warrior Queen of Matamba

### BY PATRICIA MCKISSACK

Scholastic Inc.  New York

# Angola 1595

## First Month of Mbangala: The Season When the Grass Is Burned [July 1595]

I am Nzingha. My father, who is Ndambi Kiluanji, the Ngola of the Mbundu kingdom of Ndongo, has a favorite saying: "The best way to defeat an enemy is to understand his ways." I repeat the proverb to myself each time I write in Portuguese, the language of our bitter enemy.

Although I write in Portuguese, I think in Kimbundu, the language of my people. The Portuguese are to us the Ndele, master of the white-winged birds. We gave the name to the pale visitors because their great white sails gave their ships the appearance of magnificent birds floating on the dark water. The Mbundu welcomed the newcomers, because they brought interesting things to trade. But the visitors were not true to their words of peace and love. They became invaders.

The Portuguese are not happy to rule just the Big Water.

They want to become masters of our hills and grasslands, the trees, and all the animals. They want to take what is above the ground and all that is below it. They want to lord over us. How can such a people be trusted? The Mbundu people will not be ruled by others. So we fight to keep our people and our land free. My father is away now, fighting to keep the Portuguese from pushing farther into our homeland. Even though our spies have brought us news that the Portuguese have moved their island fort of Luanda to the mainland, they have not been able to push inland. But they keep trying to build settlements on the Kwanza River.

During one of the many battles Papa Kiluanji has fought against the Portuguese, he captured Father Giovanni Gavazzi. In exchange for teaching him about the ways of the Portuguese, Papa Kiluanji spared the priest's life. This all happened before I was born — before Mukambu and Kifunji, my younger sisters, or Mbandi, our half brother, were born.

During Father Giovanni's captivity he has charmed his way into my father's confidence, and serves as one of the Ngola's advisers. Now the priest teaches Mbandi, who will probably be the next Ngola even though the boy is not bright enough to hurl a spear in the right direction. Father Giovanni is Portuguese, so I am not sure if he is a *bidibidi* (bird) or a *kulula* (a birdcage) — something harmless or something to capture our freedom.

Papa Kiluanji saw no need to provide lessons for his daughters. He hardly notices us at all. But our mother made arrangements for the priest to instruct us secretly.

I just paid the priest a measure of salt for our lesson today. If he betrays us we could all end up with our heads on poles. But that is not what troubles me. By agreeing to teach us against our father's wishes, the priest shows that he will betray Papa Kiluanji. Would he not betray him in another, perhaps more important way?

■ ▤ ■

## The Following Day

I spent the day with my friends, making arrows and dipping the heads in snake venom, the way Njali has taught us. Njali is the leader of the Chosen Ones, the royal guards, and he is with my father fighting. I miss him, because he is my friend — more like an uncle. I would love to do the things with my father that I do with Njali, but my father reserves attention for that worthless brother of mine.

Everything I know about weapons, Njali taught me. Throw your spear by extending your whole arm. . . . Never look away from your target. . . . Keep your arm straight as you pull back on the bowstring. . . . When you are in the forest, keep your bow armed with an arrow . . . and so much more. But more important than any of that, he never reminds me that I am a girl.

When it comes to Njali, my father and I agree he is the best adviser my father has. Njali, like Father Giovanni, was also a captive, taken in a battle. He is of the Imbangala people, who are from the hills south of the Kwanza River. The Imbangala used to be enemies of ours. But the Portuguese have made us allies. Njali, too, was freed, but he decided to stay with us. "Your father pays me well to fight with him," says Njali, his big voice booming. It is said that the Imbangala are loyal to the ones who pay them the most. But I know better. The kind of loyalty Njali shows cannot be bought.

Njali has been wounded so many times there is hardly a place on his body that does not own a scar. And while

Njali helps me find the right arrow feathers, I love to hear stories about how he got each wound.

## Days Later

I cannot help it, but Mbandi is such a bug. I try to be his friend, to help him run, wrestle, and throw. But instead of trying, he whines and runs away.

"Mbandi may be First Son, but he is stupid and slow, unfit to be Ngola," I tell Old Ajala. She welcomes me into her house, just outside the main gates of the city.

"Someone must be prepared to lead in Kiluanji's place," she says. "The ancestors favor you."

Next to Njali, my favorite person is Old Ajala. With only one good eye she sees more than other people see with both. She knows the secrets of this world and of the spirit world beyond, even the names of the ancestors. That is why everyone consults her before taking a journey, marrying, having children, or even building a house. When children are born, she blesses them, and when girls come of age, she presides over their presentation. Mother Kenjela says Ajala will preside over my coming-of-age presentation.

When I was just able to walk, my mother took me to Ajala for a reading. Ajala touched my head and told my mother I was destined to be the leader of Ndongo.

"But no Mbundu woman can be Ngola," Mother Kenjela said.

"Long, long ago, women were leaders among the Mbundu," Ajala answered. "It is the will of men, not the ancestors, that keeps women from becoming Ngolas. But I hear the voices of the old ones, and they say that Ndongo, the land of the Mbundu, will be ruled by a woman again."

My mother kept the words in her heart. When I was older, she sent me to Ajala for a second reading. It was the same. Since that day, Ajala has been teaching me — and now my sisters, too — about plants and herbs and the names of the ancestors. She tells us the sacred stories that are used to teach our leaders. "Your title may be lost, and your land and your servants, and even your friends will betray you, but *zai* . . . ," Ajala told me, pausing to touch her head, "*zai* — knowledge — is yours forever."

I keep all that Ajala teaches in my head. That's why when Mother Kenjela made arrangements for the priest to instruct us, I almost protested. What could I learn from the enemy? Then I remembered Ajala's words: Zai is forever.

## The Next Afternoon

Father Giovanni found me hiding near an *awunze* tree by the river. "Why are you not ready for lessons?" he asked.

I answered truthfully. "I would rather be with Njali finishing my bow or with Old Ajala learning how to make a potion that will fight off fevers."

The priest shook his head and looked disappointed.

"The day-to-day keeping of words, this diary that you gave me, is not a practice I like. What use are these pages of writing?" I asked the priest.

He chuckled softly. "Princess Nzingha, a diary is a wonderful way for people to express their innermost thoughts, make their own plans, and record their actions."

"Does the king of Portugal write?" I asked. "Does the governor of Luanda write?"

The priest shrugged. "I do not know. Probably not. Only the priests and very wealthy people are given an education in Portugal. There you would be considered a very fortunate young lady."

"We are not in Portugal. We are in Kabasa, capital of the Mbundu people," I told him. "All I need is here. What I want to know, I can ask Ajala or Njali. I have no need for a diary. Does Papa Kiluanji keep one?"

"No," Father Giovanni answered.

I could tell I had made him uneasy, but I would not stop. "If my father does not keep a diary, then pages of words cannot be too important. Why continue with this pointless exercise?"

Father Giovanni is always careful when speaking. He never talks without thinking — the consequences of having been the captive of a warrior with a fierce temper like Papa Kiluanji. After a while, Father Giovanni said, "Think about this, Princess Nzingha." He went on choosing his words slowly. "A sea captain keeps a log — a kind of diary — to tell where his caravel has visited, and what happened onboard. The logbook of Captain Diogo Cão, written over a hundred years ago, told other explorers how to find Congo and lands farther south, including your homeland here in Ndongo."

What magic is this? I was interested, as the priest knew I would be. We talked about diaries and journals. Interesting.

So here I am in the garden, writing words in a language that belongs to our worst enemy. And I do so willingly. For if these words have magic, then I will use them to plot and plan a way to drive the Portuguese from our land. And maybe one day my pages will tell others that I, Nzingha, First Daughter of Kiluanji, was a Mbundu, one of a powerful people who are free and unafraid to fight for our beloved homeland of Ndongo in the Kwanza River Valley.

## Later the Same Evening

My sisters have found me. Kifunji cannot resist teasing. She gives a big laugh. "Writing is good for you, sister. To see you sitting quietly is such a rare pleasure. Isn't it better than hurling a spear, or wrestling some boy to the ground?"

But Mukambu, my second sister, stands with me. She always does. "Nzingha's steps are longer than ours," she says, reminding little sister that I am the oldest. We are all Mother Kenjela's daughters, but we are different. Happy Kifunji loves to play, and is always busy with her hands. Quiet Mukambu is the thinker. I am accused of being independent. It is true, I suppose, for I would rather be kept in an open basket than a *lukata* — a box.

## Second Month of Mbangala: The Season When the Grass Is Burned [August 1595]

I am learning to write words on paper. But we Mbundu can send messages much faster and farther with our drums. The talking drums that pass words from drummer to drummer, village to village, tell us that Papa Kiluanji and his warriors are four sunsets out from the capital. They are camping on the Kwanza River. The Ngola is returning with a victory and many captives. The drums also say that the Portuguese have been pushed back once again. Back into the sea, I hope. As long as I have been alive, there has been war in Ndongo. I would be happy if we could have peace just for a while.

## Later

My sisters and I just returned from visiting Old Ajala. She told us a story. While we listened, our hands were busy. I strung Mother Kenjela a bracelet to wear for the Ngola's homecoming. As I selected each precious seashell, I thought of how loving our mother is to us. The bracelet tells a story of her life — a chain of sad and happy occasions.

The first shell represents young Kenjela's village in the northern hills, which was burned by the Portuguese. She was captured. The second shell reminds me that when she was being taken to Luanda to be sold as a slave, Papa Kiluanji attacked, and Mother Kenjela became a captive again.

The third shell is for the time back in Kabasa, when young Kenjela became the slave of the Ngola's mother. She missed her own mother and father, but the Ngola's mother was kind to her. The fourth shell represents Mother Kenjela as a smart and beautiful woman. When she danced she was like the wind in the tall trees. And she carried large baskets on her head with a grace that turned heads in the marketplace and caught the eye of warriors, craftsmen, and even a blacksmith. All would have been good husbands. But Papa Kiluanji is the fifth shell.

Kiluanji, the young prince of the Mbundu, wanted Kenjela as his wife. But there were many objections.

"You are the descendant of great leaders — men and women of Ndongo. As the Ngola you cannot take an outsider as your first wife," his parents argued. For each unkind comment, I added a shell.

"Kenjela is not one of us," said several of the elders.

"She is not linked to any of our ancestors," said the royal counselors.

They called Kenjela a *jaga,* which means outsider. Kiluanji was determined to have her as his bride, so he asked Old Ajala for help. The shell I used for Ajala is large and rare. She spoke to the spirits and afterward blessed the marriage. "It is the will of the ancestors," she said. Who would dare argue with that?

But to silence his parents and critics, Kiluanji married Kenjela and Kwumi at the same time. Kwumi is a Mbundu woman with all the right ancestry. Even though I think she has the heart of a pit snake, I added a shell for her and two more for Mbandi and me. Kenjela gave birth to me first, then Kwumi gave birth to Mbandi two weeks later. Although I am the oldest, Mbandi is the boy. Kwumi is First Wife. But everybody knows that Kenjela is the Ngola's beloved. I added two more shells: one for

Mukambu, who was born later, and one for little Kifunji, who was last. The bracelet is finished and so is the story.

I am almost thirteen. I have come into my womanhood, which means I am eligible to marry. At the time of the harvest, I will be presented along with all the other girls. But before I marry, I want to hunt with my father one time. But he hardly notices that he has a daughter, and besides, the Mbundu elders would forbid it.

## Later the Same Night

I am on my sleeping mat. My sisters are asleep beside me. Their breath is my breath. Their laughter is my laughter. I cannot imagine life without them. I cannot imagine life outside Ndongo.

I love the land because the land loves the Mbundu. The forested hills and valleys, the rain and sun, and our beloved Kwanza River are my father's best warriors. The forest fights intruders, confusing them, frightening them, blocking their progress. The rain makes the valleys swampy, and the sun brings the mists. And in the mists are fevers that pounce on our enemies with the fierceness of a leopard. The slow-moving Kwanza River lures the Portuguese into thinking they can ride the water into Ndongo land. But our river becomes angry, and the conquistadors are swept away on raging waters that fall down, down, down into the mists. The Ndele cannot master the land, the river, or the people, for we are the same.

## The Following Day

Soon, now, Papa Kiluanji will be here in Kabasa. I will be glad to see him, but more to my joy, I will be seeing my friend Njali. I have not hunted with him or practiced with my bow for ten full moons. The city is buzzing like a hive of bees. Inside the royal compound, the household servants have been busy getting ready for the Ngola's return. Mother Kenjela sent us with the servants to gather wild yams — Papa Kiluanji's favorite dish. Kifunji complained. "Gathering is servant's work," she said. "I am a royal princess."

Mother Kenjela scolded Kifunji softly. "You and twenty

other little girls can make that same claim. Gathering and tending the fields is women's work — strong Mbundu women's work."

My sister should not complain, but be proud that women raise the millet, beans, yams, radishes, and bananas she eats. There is no shame in knowing how to feed oneself.

Mother Kenjela has endured so much, yet my sister Kifunji is impatient and will not stand the slightest discomfort. She pricked her finger on the thorn of a wild yam. Her eyes filled with water, and she wailed as though a crocodile had snapped off her hand. When Mukambu and I showed no sympathy, she stopped crying. We laughed, and that made Kifunji angry. "Your hearts are made of iron, hammered out by the royal blacksmith," she said.

"We would be very lucky if a Mbundu blacksmith crafted any part of us," we said, laughing even harder. "Then we would be perfect."

Even our parrot knows that Mbundu blacksmiths are descendants of First Man.

When she thought about what she had said, Kifunji could not help but laugh at her own foolish self.

## The Same Evening

My sisters and I are beside each other on our sleeping mats. Papa Kiluanji is near. The drums told us that he has been advancing all day, stopping along the way to greet the farmers and herders who are his subjects. "Once they resisted him. Now they worship him," Mukambu said.

"Why is that?" Kifunji asked.

She is young, so I had to explain that the Mbundu never accepted one man as their king until the Portuguese arrived. Each village was made up of clans — families who are all kin to one another through the mothers. Each clan had its own leader, and it was to him that the villagers pledged their loyalty. Our people joined forces with our father's grandfather's grandfather, who was the first Ngola of Ndongo. The alliance of the clans has proved to be a good thing.

I told Kifunji that before I had seen nine harvests, the Portuguese governor, Dom Jeronimo, decided to attack our salt mines at Kisama. Our ally Kafushe Kambare defended the mines until Papa Kiluanji and his warriors arrived to finish the job. That was our greatest victory against the invaders. Now we have defeated Dom João

Furtado de Mendonça, who marched against the Mbundu during the rainy season. Such foolishness deserves defeat.

I love telling every detail of the story. But it must have been too long, for when I finished, Mukambu and Kifunji were sound asleep.

## Morning

Now the drums tell us that all along the way, herdsmen and farmers have put aside their work. They line the road that leads to Kabasa to sing praises and pay tribute to the triumphant army.

I was born here at the royal compound. I feel safe inside my walled city, behind the copper gates. From my window I can see most of the city. The morning sun is reflecting off the eastern gate, and I can see the green hills. Beyond is the Big Water. My eyes look at the familiar grass-roofed homes where artisans, merchants, soldiers, foreign guests, and advisers live with their families. Even if I close my eyes, I can still see the houses neatly arranged in rows that number a hundred deep on either side of the center way.

I enjoy the colorful flowers and trees that grow along shady paths and the cool pools where my sisters and I play with the other children. Since I am the oldest, I tell them stories and teach them games.

The royal courtyard where the Ngola receives his subjects is always decorated, but now it is even more festive than usual. Peacock and other bird feathers adorn each doorway. Decorating is not something I enjoy, but I helped this time. I would rather go hunting with Mukambu and Njali. Kifunji shrieks, because hunting is not the proper thing for a princess to do.

Waiting is hard.

My sisters and I are in our own personal courtyard. We are listening to the sweet song of several birds, each one trying to outdo the other. Kifunji takes care of a family of monkeys who live in our date palm tree, and Mukambu enjoys the squawking of her parrot, Ngula, which means pig. We named him that because he can imitate the sound of a pig perfectly. Whenever we go outside the compound, Ngula rides upon Mukambu's shoulder and hurls insults at real pigs from a safe distance. The little parrot wears his colorful feathers like a proud prince, but inside he is as playful as a monkey.

Across from our quarters are the rooms of the Ngola's other wives and concubines, of which there are twenty, and all their children, plus their servants and their children. This place is filled with the noises of happiness and jealousy, of love and deceit, and of good and bad. I am the oldest of the Ngola's children — thirty, at last count. Ah, I just heard the cry of a newborn. There is a royal birth in the compound almost every full moon.

## Afternoon

The waiting is too long. It is too hot to wait. But what else is there to do? I have written many words today — waiting. I did not know I had so many words inside me.

From where I am sitting I can see the corridor that leads to Papa Kiluanji's rooms. Soon he will be inside, filling them with his presence. I have never seen his chambers, but I have asked Njali to describe everything many times.

Papa Kiluanji has a sleeping mat covered with fine

white palm cloth, smooth and soft. His weapons and armor are displayed on the wall and so are charms and amulets that keep him safe. Njali says Papa Kiluanji has little else and desires nothing more except a stool and a chest. Inside the chest are the things he holds dear. No one, not even Njali, has seen them.

I imagine that looking inside that chest might be like looking inside his head and seeing his secret thoughts. Could I stand to know what he knows? Would his *zai* fill my head so full it would burst? I want to know my father and to have him know me. Oddly, my sisters do not share these feelings. It is enough for them just to be his daughters.

## Evening

More waiting. More words.

The royal compound is walled with gates that can be entered from the east and west. There are specially selected guards, the Chosen Ones. They are usually men from the royal clans whose duty is to give their lives defending the Ngola and the Ngola's family. They stand watch over us day and night.

Atandi, one of the Chosen Ones, will probably ask to be my husband when I have been presented. He comes from a strong clan, loyal to Papa Kiluanji. I have seen Atandi all my life at official ceremonies, festivals, and meetings. But he grew up in the hills, far from Kabasa. Last year he came to the capital to train as a Chosen One under Njali. I stood in the shadows to watch him practice with the spear and sword, and I am pleased that he is an able warrior, fast and agile. The idea of being married to a weak man is unthinkable.

I just wish he would smile more. My sisters say Atandi cannot smile because he would reveal his leopard's teeth. They tease me, saying that he is a leopard who, on our wedding night, will swallow me whole. When I asked Old Ajala if such a thing were true, she shook her head. "You were not meant to be a wife and mother. You will be the Ngola." That is all she will ever say. If I had my way I would not marry, but it is my duty as a royal princess to do so. Just in case, I plan to be prepared to defend myself if Atandi is, indeed, a leopard man.

When it is hard for me to sleep, like tonight, I stand watch with the Chosen Ones who were left to take care of Kabasa while the warriors are away.

## Morning

I just awoke on my sleeping mat where one of the guards brought me when I fell asleep on duty last night. A shudder just went up my back. For if I were really a Chosen One caught sleeping on duty, I would have been beheaded.

## Later

The drums tell us that Papa Kiluanji is near. I gave Mother Kenjela the bracelet I made, and told her the story of each shell. Her face glowed like the moon on a cloudless night when she placed it on her arm.

Mother Kenjela then gave the three of us bracelets for our ankles made of *banda* shells from the seacoast. Kifunji's was a double row of shells. Mukambu's shells were shaped in a circle. My bracelet was one single shell on a braided goatskin band. "One shell, because there is only one like you, Nzingha," Mother Kenjela said.

■ ≣ ■

We went out into the main courtyard to wait until it was time to assemble. While we waited we compared our newly acquired treasures. Suddenly, our brother Mbandi was upon us. I am two weeks older than my half brother, but he never lets me forget that he is the firstborn prince and that his mother is the head wife.

Kifunji and I share an equal dislike for him. We suffer his presence only when it is our duty. Mukambu feels differently and tries to defend his ways. It is one of the few things about which Mukambu and I disagree.

"Mbandi is a *lende* — a rat," I say.

"He is a little-minded boy who thinks that by strutting like a rooster he becomes one," says Mukambu. "Mbandi is to be pitied more than scorned."

Mbandi didn't bother to greet us. "I want that bracelet you are wearing, Nzingha." He reached for my arm. Without any bad intentions, I pulled away and accidentally

**25**

cuffed the boy on the head. He made a terrible piglike squeal, and Ngula the parrot heard the sound and started making pig sounds, too. We all laughed and Mbandi started bellowing like a wounded hippopotamus. As usual, his mother, Kwumi, came running.

"Nzingha slapped me for no reason," Mbandi said, burying his face in his hands.

I tried to explain. "It was an accident. He was trying to . . ."

Kwumi cut me off sharply. "Stop!" she shouted. "Nzingha, there is no excuse for your behavior. You know better than to fight with my son. The Ngola will hear of this as soon as he returns." She reminded me of a stick — rigid and thin — as she hurried away, soothing Mbandi's imaginary pain. But the boy turned toward us and mouthed the hated word . . . *jaga*. Outsider. I was ready to run into him with fists flying.

Suddenly, Father Giovanni grabbed my arm. "It is better, young princess, to be forgiving. Overlook your brother's transgressions. Turn the other cheek to anger."

I pulled away from the priest. "You forgive him!" I shouted.

My sisters gasped at my disrespect. Speaking harshly

**26**

to an elder — even a captive — is forbidden. So I apologized to Father Giovanni. He graciously accepted with a smile and a tap on the head. I wonder what thoughts are going on behind that pleasant mask he wears all the time.

## Late Afternoon

The drums are talking louder than ever. Papa Kiluanji is at the outer gates.

The market is closed. The cooks have prepared a huge feast that is ready in the compound. For now, the weavers' hands are still. The blacksmiths and their apprentices have left their forges. The advisers and royal family, servants, and slaves are gathered at the entry of the compound. Everyone has a place. Everything has a purpose.

I am filled with pride and joy. The picture of the Mbundu army and my father returning in victory will stay forever fresh in my mind. This is the way I saw it.

The royal family is positioned according to rank at the compound in the main courtyard. We are all awaiting the arrival of my father. My sisters are next to me, and our mother stands behind us. From where I am standing I see the city gates open. My heart is beating so fast I can hear it. No, it is the drumming I hear. The royal drummers enter the city first — five across and three deep. The ground upon which we stand shakes as if a blacksmith's hammer were pounding upon it.

Just as we heard the talking drums from afar, now the drummers send the message far and wide that the Ngola is in his capital city and all is well. Behind the drummers are hundreds of archers, spear throwers, and swordsmen. Then come the Ngola's Chosen Ones, of which there are fifty. Every man is said to be worth ten ordinary warriors. Njali leads them. I see Atandi's unsmiling face among them. He looks thinner than I remember. "Your husband-to-be survived," whispers Mukambu. "He must not have run away during the fighting."

I pretend not to hear her.

"Njali is home. Njali is home!" I shout. Kifunji joins me. As Njali passes, he looks fierce. Each eye is circled with white chalk and outlined in red. It is the custom of the Imbangala warriors to dress themselves in this way. But when Njali sees me a tiny smile softens his face, and I see the kind spirit that is inside my friend. And though it should never be done, I break rank and place five cowry shells in Njali's hand as a tribute. Then I thank the ancestors for protecting him against all Portuguese arrows that might have pierced his heart.

Behind the soldiers comes the Ngola himself. My father.

Papa Kiluanji stands on a platform, carried on the shoulders of fourteen men — five on each side and two at the head and back. The shouts of praise are louder than the drums.

Over his shoulder is thrown the royal leopard skin that belonged to his father and his father before him. He is also holding the ancestral spear, the second symbol of his authority, and he wears the iron bracelet, symbol of his Mbundu lineage. "He looks weary," Mukambu says. I agree. Little Kifunji does not notice a thing. She is caught up in the excitement of the whole procession. Her feet cannot be still. She dances from foot to foot and waves her hands over her head. Her joy leaps from her body to ours, and soon we, too, are dancing and jumping and swaying to the beat of the drums.

Behind the royal entourage are the captives, dozens of them stripped naked and tied together at the waist and ankles.

Once the procession reaches the gates of the compound, the drumming stops. The cheering stops. The dancing stops. The carriers lower the platform, and Papa Kiluanji kneels down and kisses the ground. Another wave of cheering spreads through the crowd.

Someone brings a handsomely carved wooden stool, another one of the great symbols of the Ngola's authority. Papa Kiluanji takes his seat and Mbandi comes and stands to the left of the Ngola, the place of the future ruler. Never has my brother looked more like a round, plump pig than today. Not strong. Not fast. Not courageous. Not even smart. Kifunji squeezes my hand. Even she notices how unkingly Mbandi appears. How could Kwumi be proud of such a son?

I cannot help but wonder what it must be like to stand in such a place of honor. I would stand as straight as a spear and make Papa Kiluanji and Mother Kenjela proud of me.

## The Next Evening

I was too excited to sleep, so once again I went out to stand guard with the Chosen Ones. I was hoping for a chance to see Atandi. Word has spread that he fought bravely during each encounter with the Portuguese, and earned the respect of his fellow warriors and especially that of the Ngola. But sadly, I've been told that Atandi has already departed for his village. I will not see him. But, no matter — I will see Atandi in due time.

As always I am quiet, for I know better than to talk to the guards while they are on duty. Instead my eyes search the darkness, watching and waiting for whatever dangers lurk there. I stay with them until weariness sends me to my sleeping mat. Instead of feeling restless, I feel relieved. Papa Kiluanji has beaten back the Portuguese. Our homeland is safe. That is as close to peace as I can hope for.

## Third Month of Mbangala:
## The Season When the Grass Is Burned
## [September 1595]

Papa Kiluanji has been home for several weeks, and I have not been able to speak to him since his victorious return. He has been receiving tribute from all the family leaders whose clan members united under Papa Kiluanji's command.

It is so good to have Njali home again. We have bothered him, pleading for stories about the battles. When he tells how the archers encircled the Portuguese, driving them deeper and deeper into the forest, I am there. When Njali describes the way the intruders are trapped with no way to get out, I am there. And when he shows us how the Portuguese cough and sweat with disease until they die, I am there and see it all. And when Njali stretches his arms out wide to show how much land the Mbundu took back from the Portuguese, I share in that victory, too. And when he finishes, I want to hear the story again and again. The only thing that would make it better would be to have really been there — in the middle of a battle, letting out a war scream that would terrify the enemy. "If I become the

32

Ngola I will go into battle with my warriors," I told my sisters.

"What warrior would follow a woman into battle?" said Kifunji.

"Not IF you become Ngola, sister, but WHEN. And never worry, I will follow you," said faithful Mukambu.

"I suppose I would, too," added Kifunji. "But only if you were losing and I had to come save the day."

## A Few Days Later

I came upon Njali this morning while he was filing his teeth into points. It is another custom of the Imbangala people. He and Papa Kilunaji have the same tallness, the same quickness of movement. But Njali has a larger head and feet. His sharp teeth make him look fierce even without war dressing.

"I have heard it said that the Imbangala kill their children," I said.

Njali shook his head. "The Imbangala are a small group compared with the Mbundu. So we live by fighting. We spread stories about ourselves, frightening stories. It seems to have worked, because we are greatly feared and hated.

33

We don't kill our children as we have told the Portuguese to do. We hide our children deep, deep in the bush so that we can move faster."

"Njali, do you miss being with your people? Your family?"

"The Ngola was my master. Now he is my friend. When I was the Ngola's slave, he allowed me to go home to my village and marry an Imbangala woman. He allowed me to keep faith with my ancestors, and he honored my beliefs and customs. I was a slave, but now I am a free man and the highest-paid warrior in the Ngola's army. This is home now. You are my family."

As we sat in the cool quiet of the courtyard, I revealed my mistrust of Father Giovanni. "He has not given me a reason to suspect him of any wrongdoing," said Njali. "But at your word, I will pay close attention to him."

## The Following Week

Kifunji was missing, so I went looking for her in the courtyard. She was in a quiet alcove beneath a plum tree, kneeling in the position in which we have often seen Father

Giovanni — hands folded, her face raised to the heavens. Did the priest teach her to do such a thing — against my father's command? I slipped away before she saw me.

When I told Mukambu what I had seen, she said it was harmless, nothing to be excited about. "Kifunji is like Ngula the parrot. She imitates."

Mukambu does not share my mistrust of the priest. Neither does Kifunji. "It is almost easy to forget he is Portuguese," said Mukambu.

I responded angrily, "You must never forget the face of the enemy."

## Several Days Later

Father Giovanni asked for and received the Ngola's permission to give the Portuguese captives something he called the body and blood of their ancestor.

When I asked Old Ajala the meaning of the ritual, she shook her beads and rattles in the four directions and chanted old words. "I have seen this done before," she said. "It is the source from which the priest gets his power and passes it on to other believers. Beware of him."

The priest is using the ritual to give the captives the power they need to . . . to do what? Why does Papa Kiluanji continue to trust this man?

## The Next Morning

I feel no larger than a *mfite* — a tiny ant. I have shamed myself before my father, my mother, visitors, even Mbandi and Kwumi.

Papa Kiluanji held court as he does every day. He had just finished settling a dispute between two merchants, when he asked if there were other complaints or petitions. To everyone's surprise, I stepped forward, asking permission to tell a story. Someone — I believe it was Mother Kenjela — tried to pull me away, for I have not been presented yet. I have no voice the Ngola is bound to honor. But my pleading eyes remained fixed on the Ngola's.

"Nzingha?" he said. He waved his hand. "Highly unusual, but I am curious. Tell your story."

It is the way of the Mbundu to criticize the Ngola by using a story. So I began. "Once there was a Leopard Ngola who ruled a great empire. It spread from where the sun rises to where the sun sets. He had a great house and many servants and warriors who did his bidding. But the Leopard Ngola had a powerful enemy — the Hyenas. The Hyenas laid traps and captured the Leopard Ngola's people. They threatened to take the Leopard's land.

"The Leopard fought the enemy with all his might, but it was getting harder and harder to defeat them. Then the Leopard Ngola took in a captive Hyena. He let him live among his people and teach his son the ways of the Hyena. Later the Leopard Ngola was attacked, and his kingdom fell because the enemy he had trusted betrayed him. What does this story mean?" I asked. Without a word of hesitation, I answered myself by pointing an accusing finger at Father Giovanni. "It is not wise to blindly trust an enemy."

Suddenly, Papa Kiluanji was standing over me, his eyes ablaze with anger. "You impudent little girl!" he shouted angrily. "Surely you have heard the Mbundu proverb, A mouse that insults the leopard should make sure she has a hole nearby."

To which I answered, "Yes, Papa Kiluanji, but there is another proverb that says, When the leopard's head is on a pole, his roar is no longer feared."

The moment I finished, I knew I had made a terrible

mistake. But I stood very straight and I refused to look frightened.

Trying to get my father's attention, I had gotten myself into serious trouble.

Then Mukambu stepped forward and took her place beside me. "I stand with Nzingha, my sister," she said.

Kifunji eased between us, slipping her small hands into ours. "So do I," she added. What a laughable sight we made, especially with Ngula the parrot perched on Mukambu's shoulders, making pig grunts.

Soft laughter spread around the courtyard. It grew louder and louder, until it was ringing in my ears. But the Ngola was as stern as ever. What was to become of us?

"In your story you made an accusation against Father Giovanni," Papa Kiluanji said. "What proof do you have that the priest is not worthy of my trust?"

I gave voice to my suspicions but avoided saying that the priest was secretly teaching us, for fear I would get Mother Kenjela in trouble. As I spoke, it became clearer that I had no proof of anything that would make the priest guilty.

"You would condemn a man to death on a suspicion?" Papa Kiluanji was furious. "You are a foolish girl, and you

**38**

have disgraced your mother, insulted me, and set a poor example for your sisters and brothers."

I looked to my mother, whose eyes were filled with a strange mixture of love and frustration. Kwumi, on the other hand, grinned as though she had unearthed a fortune. Papa Kiluanji dismissed me, yielding to the first wife, who is responsible for disciplining the royal children in court matters.

"Woman," she said, pointing to Mother Kenjela. "Come, take your daughters away. For such a display of silliness, your daughters will not be permitted to attend court for four full moons."

Mother Kenjela led us away in disgrace. What I had hoped would end with my father's recognition and respect only made things worse between us. I saw Mbandi's sneer as we passed by, and I heard people whispering, "What more can you expect of *jaga*?" What a mess I have made.

## The Same Afternoon

In our private quarters, Mother Kenjela was as angry as Papa Kiluanji had been. She scolded us. "Nzingha, your mouth will be your ruin."

Near tears, but too proud to cry, I managed to say, "I just wanted Papa Kiluanji to know me," I said.

"How can you be a leader worthy of respect if you act selfishly? You shamed yourself in front of the whole court and won no favor with your father.

"And you girls," she said, holding Mukambu and Kifunji in her gaze, "are just as silly for standing with Nzingha in her wrong." Then turning once more to me, she added, "Nzingha, you know that your sisters will follow you to the land of the dead, so you must make responsible decisions. Never lead with selfish intentions, for then all will be lost."

I had been thinking only about myself and how important I would look exposing a traitor. I may have been wrong in the way I delivered the message, but I still believe that because Father Giovanni is Portuguese, he should not be trusted.

I did not want to go to our study time, but Mother Kenjela insisted that we go and apologize to Father Giovanni. We did so, and he forgave us. "It is hard for you to understand, but even though I am Portuguese, I am not your enemy. I am a man of God, not a warrior. I am not against you. I am trying to help the Ngola in every way I know how," he said.

"You are Portuguese," I said, "yet you say you are helping my father. That makes you a traitor to your own people. I would never help my enemy, no matter what."

Mukambu and Kifunji were once again confused and shocked by my conduct. But the priest is not my concern. All I can think about is whether Papa Kiluanji will ever forgive me. I went to my friend Njali. He says that he will speak to the Ngola about seeing me privately. Tomorrow. Tomorrow I will apologize.

## The Next Evening

Njali came for me early this morning. The Ngola goes to the river to be alone with his thoughts every day. It was arranged for me to meet him there.

How many times have I followed Papa Kiluanji through the back gates that lead to the river? How often have I observed him sitting on the ground, thinking, sometimes smiling at some remembered thought, sometimes singing with the wind? And when he has left, how many times have I slipped into the place where he sat while the ground was still warm? How many dreams have I had that I was there with my father, planning some strategy or battle plan? Now I was actually there.

When I came into the Ngola's presence, I fell upon my knees and begged his forgiveness. "Papa Kiluanji, I wanted only to help, not to offend. I was disrespectful, and for that I am truly sorry."

There was a long silence.

My words must have touched the heart of the Ngola. "Rise, Nzingha," he said softly. "What you meant to do was brave — even a bit bold, standing up to me the way you did. But what you must learn now is the difference between being brave and being merely undisciplined."

My father had never spoken to me that way. I drank the words like a sweet banana drink. Had it been possible, I would have stopped the sun so the two of us could go on talking forever. "Just yesterday," he said, "you were a baby. Now you are almost a woman."

"I thought you had forgotten me."

Throwing back his head in laughter, he answered, "You are my firstborn. Forget you? Never." He leaned back for comfort. The forest was alive with buzzing. I have looked at my reflection in the quiet pools in our courtyard and noticed how much I resemble my father. I am not a beauty like my mother, but I have her strong shoulders. My eyes are my father's eyes; my nose, his nose; my laughter, his laughter; and my temper, his temper. We are alike in many ways, except I am woman and he is man. "The day you were born," Papa Kiluanji continued, "the cord that connected you to your mother was wrapped around your neck. Most babies die when this happens. But you struggled with death and won your life. That is why your name is Nzingha, which means entwined, as the vine twists and turns in the branches of a tree."

I have heard that story many times, but never in my father's voice.

Suddenly, he was on his feet. "When Old Ajala brought you to me, I knew you would be special. You are, and I will keep an eye on you — and your sisters. I admire your loyalty, one to the other. Lead them well, Nzingha." Then he was gone.

Feeling happy is better than feeling sad, is a saying we Mbundu love. It is also very true.

## Full Moon

There is a full moon tonight. It lights the forest and chases away fears. Food and dance are always very welcome in Mbundu houses, but especially when the moon is large and round and glowing.

All over, storytellers are invited to feasts and they are asked to tell the old, old stories about the ancestors who gave us our life ways.

It is a time for families to visit, to feast, and to dance, but sadly, my sisters and I are still banned from court, so there will be no celebration for us on this full moon. It is hardest on little Kifunji, because she so enjoys dancing, turning and turning and turning.


## Later

"Why aren't you ready?" Mother Kenjela scolded us. "You will be late for the royal storytelling."

"But we are banned from court," said Kifunji sadly.

Mother Kenjela told us someone spoke to the Ngola and he had pardoned us. We could go to the royal storytelling.

"Njali!" I shouted. "He must have helped us."

But Mother Kenjela said it was Father Giovanni who spoke for us.

Why does he help me, knowing I do not trust him? I wonder.

## Weeks Later

The drums announced the arrival of a visitor of some renown. Njali found a spot in court where I can see and hear. My sisters, as always, joined me today.

Papa Kiluanji received Azeze, a messenger from the southern clans of the Mbundu. They have united under a single Ngola. Azeze seemed not much older than me, though he was handsomely draped in leopard skin and feathers — a symbol of high rank. His skin was black like night, but his long hair had been reddened with mud and decorated with shells, a sure sign of his wealth. When Azeze spoke, his manner was regal, and his almond-shaped eyes were bright and alert. It was easy to see how he, though still young, had become a messenger for his Ngola. He is a prince.

Papa Kiluanji's royal seat is higher than anyone he receives. Anyone who comes before him must either sit on the floor or stand. When Prince Azeze saw that no seating would be provided for him, he called one of his servants, who knelt and formed a bench with his body. This impressed me very much. Prince Azeze wanted my father to know that he would not negotiate from a position of weakness.

Seated on the back of his servant, Prince Azeze said his father had decided to unite the clans under his authority, with Papa Kiluanji as the military leader. Papa Kiluanji agreed that the idea was sound. Then he invited Azeze to stay with us a while. I could not help but be impressed with Azeze and his regal appearance. I do not know why my heart feels happy that he is staying.

## The Following Day

Earlier my sisters and I went with Old Ajala in search of termites, a wonderful treat. Even though we complained, Mukambu brought noisy Ngula the parrot.

Always mindful that a pack of hyenas might be nearby, I kept my bow ready and armed with an arrow. By the time the sun was high in the sky, we had found a termite hill as tall as three warriors standing on one another's shoulders. As Mukambu helped raid the mound, I heard noise in the bush. Turning quickly, our guards did the same.

Something was there, watching us. Ngula's squealing had attracted a hungry leopard with a taste for pig. I saw movement to the right, but at the same time, the leopard sprang at us from the left. Suddenly, Azeze seemed to magically appear and hurled his spear at the leopard. We quickly relaxed our bowstrings. Still it was too late for the mother leopard that lay dead at our feet. Her cub was alive. It came stumbling playfully out of the bush. Without knowing, it had caused its mother's death.

"Where did you come from?" Kifunji asked Azeze.

"I was out hunting with a few men and happened to find you here. But as it appears, I did not need to save you. You princesses are quite capable."

"How did you know we were princesses?" Mukambu asked.

"I saw you at the storytelling and I inquired about you — especially you, Nzingha."

Me? Why would he be interested in knowing who I

was? I was still stunned by what had happened. I told him that if he had given it a little thought, he might not have had to kill the leopard mother. She would never have charged except to defend her cub.

"There was too little time to think," he said, looking very surprised. I could not imagine why I was so rude to him.

"There is never too little time to think," I said, pushing past him. I knew the cub would die, too, unless somebody agreed to take care of it.

My sisters had stiff words for me later.

"You are so rude and unkind," said Kifunji.

"Nzingha, Azeze saved our lives. The leopard was coming straight for us. You were not thinking clearly when you spoke," said Mukambu.

I have never been more embarrassed. All Azeze was trying to do was help us. But I will not admit that to my sisters — or tell how beautiful I think Azeze is.

Mother Kenjela chuckled softly when she heard what I had said to the visiting prince. "Sometimes," she said, "the heart sees before the eyes do."

After much begging, Ajala agreed to care for the leopard cub until it can be returned to the bush. She has warned us that only she must tend him. Ajala knows the way of animals. She can talk to them and they to her.

Tonight we ate our fill of fried termites.

## Fourth Month of Mbangala: Harvest Season [October 1595]

I have named the leopard cub Pange, which means brother. Old Ajala keeps a place for the cub near the bush. He cannot become too familiar with people, for he is a leopard. It is unnatural for him to live among men. Yet if he cannot hunt, he will die in the forest.

## Market Day

Mother Kenjela is planning for my coming-of-age dance. She took us to the market. In all of Kabasa, my favorite place is the market. You can find anything from copper jewelry to a fat snake. I love jewelry, but I don't have much good to say about snakes.

**49**

The city is full of people, mostly farmers and merchants, who have come from near and far to take part in the grand harvest festival. I am happy that even though the Portuguese have blocked the trade route from the sea, they were not able to stop the Chokwe traders from the eastern mountains, who come to trade at Kabasa. The market is more crowded than ever, with farmers who have brought their produce and artisans who proudly show off their work.

The sounds of squawking, squealing, and chattering can be heard all at once. Brightly colored fabrics dare nature to be as beautiful. And spices tickle my nose and make me sneeze and giggle at the same time. I love the smell of smoked hippopotamus meat hanging in strips and wrapped in bark. There are baskets, pottery, cloth, fish, fruits, spices, peacocks and other fowls, vegetables, livestock, and slaves.

At the far end of the market, under a canopy made of woven bark, we find Old Ajala selling her fetishes and salves. She is known for her *azewe,* a medicine made of select leaves, chalk, and mud, mixed with palm wine. It is good for fixing a sour stomach or stopping the effects of poisoning. Whatever is bad in your stomach is bound to come out after taking a big swallow of Old Ajala's cure.

Who can come away from the market without something? I found a beautiful piece of mountain zebra skin with lovely yellow-brown stripes. I will make myself a pouch for my arrows. Kifunji bought a pair of earrings, and Mukambu was pleased with a piece of cloth she liked.

Mother Kenjela has slaves who will gladly do her bidding, but she likes carrying her own basket. She fills it with manioc, large haricot beans, a palm fan, smoked goat, and bananas. Then Mother Kenjela places the basket on her head. Mukambu and I have to use our hands to keep our baskets steady. "Keep your backs straight," Mother says, teaching us gently. "Point your feet outward and swing your hips to the rhythm of your gait. That will give you the balance you need. Come follow me." We try it, and it works. Mother Kenjela begins a nonsense walking song:

> Rooster, Rooster
> Have you any bright feathers
> For sale?
> Cha ta, cha ta, chat ta
> Cha ta ta ta.

Woman, Woman,
I have no bright feathers to sell.
Cha ta, cha ta, chat ta
Cha ta ta.

## The Next Full Moon

Mother Kenjela has dressed my hair for the coming-of-age dance. It is in many braids, looped with shells. Afterward I can take my place among the women and I will be eligible to marry. Once I have been presented, an uncle of the man who wants to be my husband will speak to my father. The two will agree upon a price to be paid to my father. Because I am a princess, my father will demand a very high price — perhaps thirty goats, cloth, and weapons. As is the custom, the husband will then go and prepare a house for his bride. Then after a ceremony with feasting and sacrifices to the ancestors, the husband claims his bride.

Mukambu's face is sad. She says she will miss me. "We will still be sisters," I tell her.

She smiles. "Be happy," she says.

"Maybe Atandi will not come for you," said Kifunji. She loves to tease me.

Mother Kenjela placed an ankle bracelet on my leg. She had made it from feathers and zebra skin.

"You are ready, daughter. You are smart, brave, and strong. Now go. Dance like the lovely bird that you are."

Later, as I danced to the beat of the drums, the drummers sent the message that I, Nzingha, princess of the Mbundu people of Ndongo, had come of age. As I held up my hands to the stars and turned and turned, my father and mother watched proudly. Even Father Giovanni was there.

## Later

What a wonderful time. I can still hear the drums in my head, and I can still see the mounds of food prepared for the occasion. For the first time since I came of age, I did not have my bow slung over my shoulder.

Unsmiling Atandi managed to twist his lips upward into an almost-smile. I looked for his leopard teeth, but they did not show.

On the other hand, Azeze's smile was dazzling. "You make a perfect princess-hunter," he said.

"Then you approve of princesses who hunt?" I asked.

"Strong and smart ones, yes."

"Why not beautiful and graceful ones?"

"You amaze me, Nzingha," he said, laughing.

"Amaze you in a good way or a bad way?"

"In a very wonderful way," he said.

Azeze must think I am terrible, speaking to him in such a manner — a man I hardly know. I must be possessed by a spirit who has stolen my senses. What would Atandi think if I said those things to him? I will never know, because Atandi is not likely to say the things Azeze says to me.

To make matters worse, my sisters heard the whole conversation, and they have not stopped teasing me.

## Signal of the Rainy Season

When the large flying black bugs come, the rainy season is not far off. They fly into your hair and your food, and they get into your clothing. Fortunately, the bugs don't bite.

## Janeiro 1596:
## The Rainy Season

I am no longer a girl, yet I don't feel like a woman.

Azeze has gone home. I am glad, for I am not myself when he is around. And that troubles me. I had almost forgotten my one wish — to hunt with my father before I marry. It feels good to have my bow slung over my shoulder again, if only for a little while longer. I will enjoy this time. Maybe there will be time to hunt with Papa Kiluanji. I have spoken to Njali about my wish. If he can help, he will, I know.

Father Giovanni is teaching us the strange way the Portuguese measure the passage of time. Seven days make a week. Weeks become months. Twelve months make a year. Today begins Janeiro, the first month of the year 1596. It all seems so complicated. Here among the Mbundu there is night. There is day. There is a time to plant. There is a time to harvest. There are the phases of the moon. What need have I of weeks, months, and years?

But I must admit, Father Giovanni was right. I do enjoy writing in my book of words. So perhaps as I use them

**55**

more, I will become more comfortable with the names of days, weeks, months, and years.

## The First Week of Janeiro

All the princes and princesses gathered in the outer courtyard to hear a teaching tale told by the royal storyteller. But before we finished, Papa Kiluanji sent for Mbandi to join the hunt.

Right away the boy whined and complained that his stomach hurt. I knew he was faking, so I suggested that he might need a swallow of Old Ajala's azewe cure. Mbandi immediately said it was his bow arm that hurt and not his stomach. Silly boy. He hates hunting.

Njali gestured for us to follow him. "Not me," said Kifunji. "I want to hear the rest of the story." Mukambu and I leaped to our feet.

"I might be able to help," Njali said, leading us to a clearing in the bush. There he told us to stay and practice shooting our arrows, and he would bring the Ngola to us. The Ngola would think he had met us by chance. Njali is wonderfully cunning.

Soon I heard footsteps. I made my arrow true to its mark. Mukambu's arrow zinged to a spot so near my own, it was as if they were only one arrow.

"What is this, Njali?" Papa Kiluanji asked, stepping into the clearing. "These girls would put most of my archers to shame. And to think," he said, smiling, "they are my daughters. Who taught you to use the bow so well?"

"Njali," we answered. Papa Kiluanji nodded his approval, and told us that Imbangala women were superior archers and that Njali had trained us in their tradition. Papa Kiluanji turned to go. I asked him to stay, talk for a while. "Tomorrow, after we return from hunting, I will send for you," he said.

"Why can't we go hunting with you now?" I asked.

Mukambu gasped softly. I knew what she was thinking. I had done it again — said the wrong thing. I closed my eyes not knowing what to expect.

A few of the men grumbled that no Mbundu women ever accompanied them hunting. As always, Papa Kiluanji listened to all good counsel. Then he made his decision.

"Long ago, Mbundu women hunted with the men," he

said. "It is time we reinstated that custom. My daughters are coming with us."

And after all the years of yearning, I finally got my wish.

## The Second Week of Janeiro

Things have changed rapidly since I went hunting with Papa Kiluanji. He has spent more time with us than ever before. Just this morning, he spoke with Father Giovanni. We are going to be allowed to study along with Mbandi. "Now you don't have to learn in secret any longer," he told us, smiling at Mother Kenjela.

"You knew all along that we were getting lessons from Father Giovanni?" I asked.

"I would not remain Ngola very long if I did not know what was going on under my own roof."

"Njali must have told you," I said. "He is so loyal to you."

"No. It was Father Giovanni who told me."

I do not understand this priest. Could I be so wrong about a person and not realize it?

# Fevereiro:
# The Second Month of 1596

It has been raining for days and days. Even when it is not raining, the air is thick with water. The nights are steamy hot, and it is hard to breathe. The rains also bring the fevers that steal away life. It is especially hard on the old ones and babies. Mother Kenjela, like all good mothers, keeps us protected with amulets and herbs.

Rain or not, Mbundu men must hunt. I join the men as often as I can, loving every minute of our time in the forest. The men who resented my presence in the beginning are now among the first to ask about me when I am absent.

Papa Kiluanji is especially pleased with my skill. We have hunted crocodiles, birds, and other animals. Just this morning, we killed a hippopotamus. When it was skinned, I was allowed to take one of its teeth. I will grind the tooth into a powder, which Old Ajala says wards off evil fevers that steal the life of sleepers. This time with my father is better than I could ever have imagined possible.

## Março:
## The Third Month of 1596

The rains have stopped and the forest is in full bloom. My favorite blossom is the Moonflower, which opens in moonlight. All around us is a feast of color and sounds. Here, human hands cannot reproduce the Earth Mother's handiwork. But in all this beauty, the threat of the Portuguese lurks in the shadows.

Traders from the North came to warn us that small bands of raiders are in Ndongo. They have burned one Mbundu village and set traps for travelers along our borders. Papa Kiluanji will not tolerate raiding in his territory, so he has ordered Njali to lead a group of Mbundu warriors against a *presidio*, a fort on the Kwanza River just above the falls. It is only a matter of time before the Portuguese find a way to get beyond the great forest into Ndongo lands. Only the Mbundu can stop their advances.

## Weeks Later

Njali is back home. The drums told us two days ago that he was returning with a victory. The presidio has been destroyed, and several slavers taken as captives. Who can stand before our Mbundu warriors? But our old friend seems changed somehow. He is quieter, and he goes away for long periods. He hardly spends time with us anymore. What is the matter, I wonder? What could it be?

## Later

After I attended lessons with Father Giovanni, I hurried to spend time with Old Ajala and the leopard cub, Pange.

The cub stays in the bush away from human beings, except Ajala. We leave fresh kill for him daily. Even I do not touch Pange or play with him, though it is difficult. I want him to remain a part of the forest. "The cub is a leopard and it is his nature to roam free," I tell Kifunji, who wants to hug his neck. As soon as he is large enough, Ajala will leave him to hunt for himself. But for now, I understand the temptation to embrace such a beautiful creature.

## The Following Day

Now that the rains are over, the people of Kabasa are busy repairing their houses, adding fresh grasses to the roofs. Old vines that covered the walkways have been cut back to allow new growth. Fresh feathers are attached to everything. It is a good time. The rains have passed, and new life is sprouting from the ground.

In the marketplace, women carry their young babies in animal skins adorned with magical charms. They know that if the spirits who dwell in the mists are angered, they will steal a baby in the night. Angry spirits also cause troubles, ranging from insect bites to sprained ankles to crop failure. So we are all careful with every word we say, lest a misspoken deed wakes up an angry *diabu* — a bad spirit.

## Later

Now that I am getting to know Papa Kiluanji, he has been spending a lot of time with me. He gives me his *zai* as we sit by the river almost daily. "Soon you will be married and in the house of your husband," he said. "If I had heeded the prophecy about you, I would have started instructing you long ago, but I had an obligation to my son."

"As long as you live, Papa Kiluanji, the kingdom is safe."

"But I will not last forever. My body tires even as I speak. You must promise me something. Your brother is weak, and there are those who will try to use him to gain power."

He asked me to promise that I would not allow Mbandi to destroy the kingdom with his weakness. That I would take control, and be a leader worthy of following. "Remember," he said, "the ancestors chose you."

I promised my father that I would do as he asked.

Here in the quiet of our courtyard I am sifting my father's words through my mind. He has given me his blessing to rule Ndongo when the time comes.

## Days Later

Since our talk, Papa Kiluanji has been allowing me to stand at his side when he is holding court. I used to wonder what it would feel like to stand here, next to him. Now I am here, and I like it.

Kwumi is spreading rumors and whispering that with

the help of Old Ajala, we have witched Kiluanji into favoring us over Mbandi. I don't care what she thinks.

More important than Mbandi and Kwumi are the elders. They are concerned about Papa Kiluanji's intentions regarding my position. But they dare not question his authority or his decisions. Instead they grumble their dissatisfaction among themselves. Papa Kiluanji told me later that Mbandi's uncles are helping to spread the rumors. "They must be watched. They are men who crave power," he told me at our special place by the river. "And they will do anything to gain the power they seek."

Later, I told Mother Kenjela what Papa Kiluanji has been telling me. Kwumi's brothers remind me of crocodiles disguised as fallen limbs — always watching, always waiting for someone to make a mistake so they can pounce.

Mother Kenjela hugged me. "Daughter," she said, "I think we put too much on your shoulders. But remember, you have sisters who are always willing to help you."

"Always," said Mukambu.

"Maybe I will," said Kifunji, giggling. Then turning around and around beneath a cloud of cloth, she announced, "Maybe I won't."

## Abril:
## Fourth Month of 1596

Where is Njali? He has been gone for days — weeks. Where does he go? There are rumors that he is off somewhere fighting for hire. I miss him.

## Afternoon on the First Day of the Week: Domingo

Njali is home. But he has not come to see us. That is strange. When I did see him, I asked where he had been.

"To see my aging mother," he said.

For the first time in my life I do not believe Njali. Why? "He told us his mother was dead," Mukambu reminded me.

Why would Njali not speak the truth about such a thing? What is he hiding?

## Terça-feira

My sisters and I were in the forest looking for wild yams, when we heard sounds in the distance. We hid behind a fallen *awunze* tree. Two men passed not an arm's length from where we were hiding, but they did not see us. They were dressed as Portuguese. They spoke Portuguese. But they were black. I wanted to know who these men were. Where had they come from and why were they in Ndongo?

I did not think they would be much of a match against Mukambu and me. We could take them, especially since we had the element of surprise on our side.

Quickly, I shared a plan with my sisters. When Mukambu and I charged, Kifunji made noise, making it sound as though there were more of us. Then I gave out a war cry and rushed forward, arrows flying. The cowards offered no resistance, but fell on their knees in submission. We tied them fast with forest vine and proudly marched our two captives to the royal city. We turned them over to Njali.

## The Next Day
## Quarta-feira

By the time the Portuguese captives were presented to the Ngola, they had changed into the dress of Congo men from the north. Njali called them *Pombeiros* — men whose mothers are black and fathers are Portuguese. They learn the ways of their mother's people, then use the *zai* — knowledge — to help their fathers capture slaves. They are slave traders who work with the Portuguese.

"Your borders are safe as long as you have warriors as fierce as these," one of the Pombeiros said, bowing to my sisters and me.

"We are honored to be in the presence of the great Kiluanji, Ngola of the Mbundu people of Ndongo," said the other.

Papa Kiluanji was not flattered or amused. "You wanted to be brought here. Before you are executed, please tell me for what purpose you have forfeited your lives."

The Pombeiros immediately requested a private audience. Papa Kiluanji agreed.

Later, with my sisters, I shared my disgust that the Pombeiros had allowed us to capture them. It was a game — not a true test of our battle skills.

As I talked, the whole encounter took on a strangeness. How did those two men get so close to our capital without

being noticed? I felt they had to have had help. As I re-
lived the encounter in my head, it seemed familiar. Then
it came to me. Our meeting with the Pombeiros was the
same as when Njali planned our meeting with Papa Kiluanji the first day we went hunting with him. It had looked
like a chance meeting, but in reality Njali had arranged it
all. What is he up to? I am concerned but I am not about
to let my suspicious nature hurt the best friend I have.

## A Day Later
## Quinta-feira

The two Pombeiros are still talking with Papa Kiluanji.
No one knows what they are discussing. Mukambu and I
have tried every way we can think of to spy on the talks,
but without Njali's help we can't get close.

We were all summoned to court earlier today. The
drums said the Ngola was going to make an important
announcement.

To everyone's surprise, Papa Kiluanji said that the

Portuguese governor, Dom João Furtado de Mendonça, had sent the two Pombeiros with an offer to negotiate a peace agreement. The Portuguese will cease all efforts to develop permanent settlements if the Mbundu will agree to provide slaves. The governor invited Papa Kiluanji to a meeting in Luanda to discuss the terms in more detail.

Peace for slaves? Could peace be achieved so easily?

"What do you think of this?" Papa Kiluanji asked Mbandi.

The boy looked at his mother, then his uncles. His eyes blinked. "I — I think it is a trick to capture you." Everybody nodded in agreement.

"What do you think, Nzingha?" he asked.

"I agree with Mbandi. He is right," I answered, knowing that I did not. Yes, capture was possible. But the Ngola would not let peace slide from his hand without trying to grasp it. To disagree with Mbandi in the open at court would only make it more difficult between us, though. I will speak my real feelings to the Ngola later.

The Pombeiros were told the following: "Go to your governor and tell him that Kiluanji, Ngola of the Mbundu people, will not come to Luanda to negotiate a peace."

The Portuguese know that the capture of one man —

even the Ngola — would not destroy the will of the Mbundu people to fight on. No. The Portuguese are up to something. Can it be as simple as slaves for peace? Slaves are everywhere. What do they really want, and in what way is Njali involved in this matter?

## Later

My answer came sooner than I thought. In the middle of the night, Njali came for me. Papa Kiluanji wanted an audience.

"Get prepared," my father said. "You leave for Luanda in the morning. Njali and Father Giovanni, whose freedom I have granted, will accompany you and a few of my most trusted Chosen Ones. I am also releasing all the Portuguese captives I have as a gesture of goodwill."

To Luanda. I was too overwhelmed to speak.

I would meet with the governor on my father's behalf and bring him the details of the discussion. Then he would make his next move.

When Njali and Father Giovanni left the room, my father and I talked — just the two of us. "I knew when you agreed with Mbandi that you were mature enough to handle the job before you. You would be my eyes and ears. I trust you. Are you frightened?"

"No." I was truthful. Fear never entered my mind. Surprise, yes. I was concerned about my father's two other choices, and with permission to speak freely, I expressed my concerns. "You know that I have never trusted Father Giovanni. But lately, I have had cause to wonder about our beloved friend Njali. And please don't ask me to offer proof of any wrongdoing. I have none — just my feelings."

Papa Kiluanji opened his treasured chest. "Treachery lives among us," he said. "But this trip is a test to see whom I can really trust." Then he gave me a piece of royal cloth. "Drape yourself in this and shine like the royal princess that you are."

"I will not fail you," I answered.

"Remember all I have taught you."

## Junho: The Sixth Month of 1596

I have not written in weeks because I have been to Luanda and back. Now I must take time to write the words or I will forget all the many things I have seen and heard.

**71**

After tearful good-byes with Mother Kenjela and my sisters, we departed Kabasa while the morning birds were chirping but before the sun had come fully awake. At first we traveled by dugout along one of the many tributaries that form the Kwanza River. Seeing things with a new eye, I drank in the sights like a thirsty man. Green papyrus with fingered tops lined the banks. A big hippopotamus slid into the water and disappeared. Water birds, too many to count, fed in the shallows, watchful for the crocodiles that eyed them from a distance.

When the water became swifter, we hugged the banks, but we had to dodge low-hanging branches and birds' nests. Njali spied a herd of impala, ranging in color from dark brown to black, and pointed them out to me. Father Giovanni was amazed at their enormous horns. I was delighted to see a zambu draped over the river. A zambu is formed by the branches of trees on one side extending to the branches of trees on the other side, which makes it possible to swing across the river without touching the water.

Days passed mile after mile. The way was rugged and hard. At last the forest gave way to grasslands, and then to the coastal desert.

Finally, we came to Luanda and entered the mouth of the lion.

It is time to go to the market with my sisters. I will tell more of the story later.

## The Next Day

I have a few minutes before it is time to attend court. I will use the time to write more of my experience in Luanda.

We made our way to the governor's great compound — a place the Portuguese call a palace. We were welcomed by one of the pombeiros who had been at Kabasa. He greeted us and graciously showed us where we were to stay during our visit. Weary from weeks of travel, I slept that first night without stirring.

Early the next morning, I wanted to go outside my room to find Njali, but a guard there would not let me pass. At first I was frightened, thinking that I was a prisoner. But the slave girl, Susanna, who brought food, was Mbundu. She assured me that I was not a captive. No guests were allowed to roam about the palace freely.

So I sat in the window that overlooked the sea, looking at the ships come and go at the will of the wind and water.

I smiled as I thought to myself that the sails did look like huge bird's wings. No wonder my people call the Portuguese "Ndele."

"Where do the big ships go?" I asked Susanna in Portuguese.

She was shocked that I could speak Portuguese. "Portugal and a land called Bra-zil," she answered.

"Have you ever been to any of those places?"

"No, but I know a man — a Mbundu — who is the captive of a Portuguese ship captain."

"Could you arrange for me to meet this man?"

Susanna promised that she would try.

The drums are calling me to court. I must put away the writing for now.

## The Next Day Morning

It is early morning, a good time to write. I will pick up the story where I stopped.

Days passed, but the governor of Luanda did not receive us. Every morning Susanna came and helped me drape myself in the fine cloth my father gave me. In the afternoon, I returned to my room, removed the cloth, ate alone, then went to sleep. If it had not been for Susanna, the waiting would have been miserable.

One afternoon as I returned from another day of waiting, Susanna pulled me aside. Taking me to the kitchen, she introduced me to another Mbundu man named Juan Pedro. "This is Nzingha, First Daughter of Kiluanji, Ngola of Ndongo," Susanna said.

Juan Pedro explained that his name was Jmee, but that he had been baptized and renamed by his master, who was a sea captain.

I wanted to know only one thing. "What happens to the captives when they leave this place?" I asked.

"They go to Brazil to work on the tobacco and sugarcane plantations."

Tobacco? Sugarcane? Plantations? We talked for a long while, Juan Pedro explaining to me what these new words meant. He said that every ship that left Luanda was filled with people, many of them Mbundu captives taken in battles. Day after day, hundreds of them were put in the belly of the ships. "You can hear them wailing, crying out, begging for mercy. But there is no mercy. Some try to fight. Some wish to die and hurl themselves into the sea where their souls can fly back to their homeland and be free. For days the ship travels over the Big Water until they come to Brazil. There they are made to work in the fields until they drop. Then new ships come with fresh captives who take their place."

After hearing this report, I made up my mind that I wanted no part of the Portuguese slave trade. I also knew I would counsel Papa Kiluanji to have nothing to do with it either.

Later, as I slipped back to my room, I saw Father Giovanni speaking to one of the pombeiros in the corridor. When they thought no one was looking, Father Giovanni gave him a small sack — gold, most likely. The Portuguese love gold more than any other material that comes from the ground. What was the priest buying?

The next morning, we went to the governor's receiving hall as usual. But that day, a small man with a bird-beak nose called us. He was sweating, his thick clothing was dirty, and he smelled of sour goat's milk. "Things have not changed since I've been away. A bribe still works," Father Giovanni whispered as we were announced to the governor. So that is what he had bought. I guess I had the priest to thank again.

"Princess Nzingha," said Governor Mendonça, "I will make an offer plain and simple for you to understand. . . ."

Remembering Azeze and how impressive he had been at my father's court, I interrupted. "Please excuse me. Is there a chair?"

"Bring the princess a mat to sit on," Governor Mendonça said impatiently.

But on the floor, I would have been below the governor, who was seated in a chair. I did not want to negotiate from a position of weakness. I called for one of the guards who attended us. Whispering to him what I wanted him to do, he willingly obeyed. He bent over and made a bench. Seated upon his back, I motioned for the governor to continue. Clearly, he was as baffled as I knew he would be. I was young, but I was not a child.

Governor Mendonça said he wanted the Mbundu to deliver to him five hundred slaves — men, women, or children — two times a year. "They will be used to work our fields and perform household duties." He said nothing about Brazil or the long trip across the Big Water.

"Where are we to get that many captives twice a year?" I asked.

"You have enemies. Capture them," he said. "We

guarantee that your father will be paid well for his services. You will also be the masters of your land, free of enemies, and you will have peace." Then the governor added that he wanted priests and monks to be allowed to preach the "holy word" and "baptize" freely in Ndongo. There was one more thing the governor added, peering at me from under bushy eyebrows. He wanted to set up forts along the Kwanza River and at Massangano.

Forts? This was the first time any more presidios had been mentioned. When I objected, he said the rest of the agreement was off unless the forts were acceptable. "I will await the Ngola's response," he said.

Graciously, I agreed to take the offer to Papa Kiluanji. Then he dismissed us without ceremony.

Before I was escorted to my room, I managed a moment with Njali. I shared what I had learned about slavery as it was practiced in the place called Brazil. "We treat our livestock better. I will report what I have seen and heard to Papa Kiluanji. He should know these things before he agrees to deliver captives to these people," I said.

Njali reminded me that slavery was not new to us. He had been a slave. My mother had been a slave. "We have always sold our captives," he said. "It is the way of the Mbundu. The difference now is that we will sell them to the Portuguese for much wealth — and wealth is power."

"No, the difference now is that the child of a slave is born a slave. That is not the Mbundu way. I will use my influence to get my father to turn away from this agreement."

Njali backed away. "You're making a mistake, Princess," he said. "Much is at risk here. The profits are too good to ignore."

"But it is not just about profits," I said, wondering more and more about my old friend. Why was he defending this wretched curse the Portuguese were calling slavery?

It pains me to write more at this time. I must pause to collect myself.

## Several Days Later

Writing about what happened in Luanda helps, but it still makes my heart heavy.

From my window I watched a ship, its shape dark against the late evening sky. Its large white wings were tucked in a position of rest, but there was plenty of activity on shore. As

I looked more closely, I saw people being shoved into small boats and rowed out to the larger ship. Some of them were girls who looked like me, Mukambu, and Kifunji. It is not just about profits, I told myself.

I wondered what it must be like to be on a ship flying over the water to Brazil. The horror of it was beyond my understanding.

Suddenly, there was noise at my door. The Pombeiros and several guards entered. "Come with us." Then speaking to the guards, one said, "Hold her tight. She is a young leopard."

I fought back and tried to escape. But I was caught and pushed down the corridor, out the door, beyond the white walls of the palace, and into the street. There, I was handed over to another man, who quickly put a sack over my head and held me tightly.

One of the Pombeiros said, "Thank you for the warning. With her out of the way, our plans will go as expected. We will all be wealthy with kingdoms of our own."

Who was he thanking? I jerked my arm away and snatched off the sack. There stood Njali.

"The Ngola will have your head for this," I said, feeling more hurt than angry.

Njali laughed. "This is the way it is, Princess. Loyalty to the highest bidder. Enjoy your trip."

I spat at him.

I was grateful when they put the sack over my head again, so that they would not see the tears flowing from my eyes. My hands were tied, but I would not be led like a goat.

Then came shouts, a scuffle, more shouts. In the struggle, I was pushed to the ground and bumped my head. I was knocked out. When my eyes focused again, I saw Father Giovanni leaning over me. I was safe among his brethren in a secret place. "You have never been in any danger, Princess, because one of the brethren has been watching out for you."

Those had always been Njali's orders — to protect me with his life. Now I was being protected by my enemy.

"Why do you help me?" I asked the priest.

"I owe this to your father for all his kindness and because he trusted me," he said. The priest explained that Njali had been working with the Pombeiros all along, but he had been assured that the governor was not involved in the scheme to sell me.

"How could Njali be so corrupt without us knowing it?"

"You must let me tell you the story of Judas someday," Father Giovanni answered.

The priest escorted me to the border of Ndongo land. There he turned back.

"I have been so cruel to you, Father Giovanni. For this I am sorry." I begged him to come back to Ndongo. "There is so much more I need to learn."

"I taught you a good lesson, Nzingha: Not all Portuguese are your enemy," he said. "Maybe one day I will return to Kabasa. But for now, I can do more good here."

After living among the Mbundu for so many years, he had come to believe that what his people were doing was wrong. "Maybe I can get the governor to listen to me. And just maybe a real peace can be obtained."

I reported everything that happened to Papa Kiluanji in the words as I have written them.


## The Following Morning

It is good to sleep beside my sisters again, listening to them breathe in and out, in and out. They heard the story of my adventure, and then they wanted to hear it again.

As I lie here on my sleeping mat, I cannot believe so much has happened in such a short time. Mother Kenjela has draped me in words of praise. She says I wear them well.

It is good to have my bow over my shoulder again. It is also good to be home among people I love and trust. The idea of being taken to Brazil still makes me feel dizzy.

## The Next Night

After a day with Ajala and Pange, I am tired. The heat does not bother me, but tonight I could not sleep, so I went to stand guard with the Chosen Ones. As I rounded the corner, I caught a glimpse of a shadow figure springing over the wall and down the corridor to Papa Kiluanji's quarters. Thinking that some stranger was up to mischief, I armed my bow and followed. Rushing it to warn my father, I was shocked to find Njali standing there.

"You!" I shouted. "You traitor."

Papa Kiluanji threw up his hands. "Stop, Nzingha. It is not what you think."

To my joy, Njali is not a traitor. He is a perfect spy. For

months he has been working with the Pombeiros, making plans that would make him appear to be a traitor. My capture was all planned, too. Njali wants to make the Pombeiros think he is against us. In this way he will learn about future slave raids, where the Portuguese are planning to build new forts, and who among us is working for them.

"We did not tell you our plans, Nzingha," said Papa Kiluanji, "because we wanted your struggle to be real."

"We did not tell Father Giovanni, either, because we wanted his rescue to be real," added Njali.

"Never let the right hand know what weapon the left hand is holding," I said, remembering Papa Kiluanji's favorite proverb.

"You were never in any danger, Nzingha," said Njali. "I would defend you to the death."

"I will never doubt you again — even when my eyes tell me one thing, my heart will know better."

I am happy now — content that my friend is still my friend. I am happy that Father Giovanni is really a good man who believes in his ancestors' teachings. I am pleased that my father has made me one of his trusted advisers. But most of all I am happy that he is not going to make an agreement with the Portuguese to sell slaves.

## Setembro:
## Full Moon 1596

Mother Kenjela is making plans for Mukambu's presentation. I remain unmarried. Papa Kiluanji has sent for me. I will write more later.

## Later

"I have received a bride offer for you," he said. "A very large bride offer. One of the largest I have ever heard of. In my opinion it is still not enough for a daughter such as you."

I could not contain my smile. "When is Atandi coming for me?"

"It is not Atandi who makes the offer. It is Azeze."

I am not disappointed about Atandi. With Azeze I will not have to put up my bow and arrows when I marry. And maybe I will not miss hunting with my father, because I will be hunting with my husband. The idea makes me giggle, and I have not giggled in a long, long time. I must go now to tell my sisters and Mother Kenjela the good news.

# Epilogue

Between 1596 and 1617, Nzingha married and gave birth to a son. Unfortunately, her husband Azeze was killed in battle a few years later. Nzingha never gave up hunting and was often seen leading a group of hunters — both men and women — her bow slung over her shoulder. Mukambu and Kifunji were also married and widowed by war, but they continued to be Nzingha's constant companions.

Ngola Kiluanji never formed an alliance with the Portuguese, but other groups did. With the help of the Pombeiros — men with black mothers and Portuguese fathers — and those allies who joined them, the Portuguese were able to invade deep into Ndongo territory. Thousands of people were taken captive and ended up working until they died of exhaustion in Brazil or on

Caribbean islands. Even though the Mbundu fought to protect their homeland, they were losing ground. Mbundu warriors suffered a tremendous defeat at Massangano in 1597. Kiluanji was severely wounded but did not die. The Portuguese discovered that Njali was a spy and sentenced him to be hanged. He escaped, however, and made his way back to Kabasa, where he continued to fight alongside Kiluanji. Worse times were yet to follow.

Kiluanji died in 1617, and Mbandi's uncles helped him seize power as the Ngola. Crazed by power, he ordered the murder of all those who opposed him, including Mother Kenjela and Nzingha's only son. Mbandi would have killed Nzingha, but she was too popular with the people.

Nzingha did everything she could to keep the promise she had made to her father. She put her personal feelings aside when Mbandi asked her to go to Luanda to negotiate a treaty. There would be time for revenge.

Once again in Luanda, she refused to be seated on the floor and called for a servant to create a human bench. Then, seated upon a servant's back, she negotiated a peace agreement. While in Luanda she reestablished contact with Father Giovanni and was baptized. She took the name Ana de Sousa to honor the new governor, Fernando

João Carreida de Sousa. Many people questioned her motives. Those who knew her best reported that she allowed herself to be baptized out of respect for Father Giovanni and his loyalty to her father, but also it was to her advantage in dealing with the Portuguese. It gave her time to establish herself as a leader.

Weeks after Nzingha returned to Kabasa, Mbandi was dead. The Portuguese felt it was time to attack Kabasa. After years of poor leadership, Kabasa was burned. Nzingha and her people fled to the mountains where she rallied the remnants of her army. It was at this moment in history that Nzingha took control.

In 1624, at the age of 42, Nzingha became Ngola Kiluanji of the Mbundu people of Ndongo — just as Old Ajala had predicted on the day she was born. Always at her side were her sisters, Mukambu and Kifunji. Njali, who remained her friend, helped Nzingha forge an alliance with the Imbangala. And for the next forty years she waged a war against the Portuguese slave trade from the rocky slopes of Matamba.

The Portuguese captured Mukambu and Kifunji. But with the help of slaves in Luanda, they escaped. Kifunji was later killed in battle.

Nzingha led many battles and negotiated peace treaties with the Dutch and Portuguese for many years. But she never gave up her resistance against slavery. Living to be eighty-two years old in the forested hills she called her home, Nzingha died in 1663. Her sister, Mukambu or Doña Barbara (her Christian name), took over the leadership of the Mbundu people in Matamba. Mukambu ordered that her sister, Ngola Nzingha Kiluanji of Matamba, was to be laid to rest covered in her leopard skin. And in defiance of the Portuguese, she had a bow slung over her shoulder and arrows placed in her hand.

# Life in Angola in 1595

# Historical Note

Probably the most informed chronicler of Nzingha's life was Father Giovanni Gavazzi, a Portuguese priest who lived in Ngola Ndambi Kiluanji's court for years. He also wrote most of what we know about Nzingha's father from which Nzingha's young life was reconstructed. Unfortunately, Gavazzi's understanding and interpretation of African customs and beliefs was filled with stereotypes and biases that persist to this day. More contemporary writers and African historians have used what Gavazzi wrote and tried to separate fact from fiction, allowing the real Nzingha to emerge. Every attempt has been made to be accurate in the research and retelling of this version of Nzingha's life.

The people, places, customs, and events in the diary are historical. Even the fictional characters are realistically portrayed based on people who were part of Nzingha's life. Nzingha's visit to Luanda, however, did not take place when she was thirteen. The only such visit recorded took place in 1622. At the age of 40, Nzingha was sent to Luanda by her brother to negotiate a peace treaty with the Portuguese (two years after the Pilgrims had landed at Plymouth in Massachusetts Bay Colony, and three years after the first African captives were sold at Jamestown, Virginia Colony). It was then that Nzingha used the back of a servant as a bench to speak to the Portuguese governor.

While Nzingha was in Luanda, she was baptized and named Doña Ana de Sousa. Historians have questioned her reasons for accepting Christianity, for nothing ever indicated that she practiced it as her primary religion. Whether it was a legitimate conversion or a way of playing up to her Portuguese adversaries is not known.

The Portuguese had been trying to break the resistence of the Mbundu people since explorer Diogo Cão reached the mouth of the Congo River in 1483. The Congo at that time included the area that is now the country of Angola. For a while the Portuguese maintained peaceful relations with the Congo leaders, trading slaves for weapons. But as the Portuguese slave traders moved South and became more violent and intrusive, they met with resistance. Nzingha's grandfather, Ngola Mbandi Kiluanji of Ndongo refused to accept Christianity or Portuguese colonization.

When Paulo Dias de Novães visited Kabasa in 1561, the Ngola held him hostage for four years. When Novães returned to Lisbon, Portugal, he reported to King Sebastiao that the only way to defeat the Mbundu was through military action. Novães returned to Congo and established himself governor of Luanda in 1576. Luanda was the seat of the Portuguese colonial administration and a primary slave trading port.

For over forty years the Portuguese had been unable to penetrate the interior of Angola. Naturally, the Portuguese were hopeful that a "Christianized" Nzingha would allow them to expand. They were mistaken.

Nzingha shrewdly used her alliance with the Portuguese to seize power from her incompetent brother. Driven mad by his power, Mbandi had destroyed all hope of an alliance among the various people of the region. Fighting disrupted the trade route, and farmers who spent more time as warriors did not produce bountiful harvests.

Shortly after Nzingha's return from Luanda, the Ngola was dead. Although Nzingha was suspected, it was never proven that she killed or had her brother killed. She denied it, suggesting that he committed suicide. There is little evidence left to draw any conclusions one way or the other. First Nzingha was appointed regent, then Queen of Ndongo in 1624. To secure peace for her people, Nzingha paid the Portuguese taxes of slaves and ivory.

Slowly, Nzingha began backing away from her pact with the Portuguese, and defiantly refused to supply her quota of slaves or to allow colonization on Mbundu land. The Portuguese retaliated by attacking Kabasa and burning it in 1629. Fleeing to the hill country of Matamba, Nzingha represented those Mbundu people who opposed the Portuguese.

Her beloved Ndongo came under the control of the Portuguese. They selected a puppet Ngola, Ari Kiluanji, to rule the Mbundu people. Some of the Mbundu clans followed him but others refused, joining Nzingha in the hills above the Kwanza River Valley. Thus, the Mbundu people were divided. Ari Kiluanji agreed to provide all the slaves the Portuguese requested in exchange for peace, but Nzingha steadfastly refused to participate in the slave trade. She offered all runaway slaves sanctuary. These fugitives were a major component of her "*jaga* (outsider) army."

Refusing to be stopped, Nzingha conquered the kingdom of Matamba, where she formed an alliance with the Imbangala, who had no problem in accepting a woman Ngola. Nzingha was acquainted with Imbangala warriors in her father's court and they became the core of her volunteer army.

From 1630 to her death in 1663, Nzingha, Queen General of Matamba, launched a formidable opposition to the Portuguese regime. She also welcomed all *jaga*. Anyone willing to take up arms against the Portuguese was recruited.

Nzingha is known primarily for her military battles against the Portuguese in Angola. Yet, she was troubled because she was never able to unify the Mbundu people. Throughout her career the Mbundu clan chiefs, or *sobas*, never accepted her authority. Her sex was a disqualifying factor, as was her lack of Mbundu lineage (traced through the mother). Those elements, combined with rumors that

**97**

Nzingha had killed her predecessor made it impossible for her ever to be accepted. Yet she ruled for almost forty years in both Ndongo and Matamba with astonishing military skill and diplomatic savvy.

When the Dutch occupied Luanda from 1641 to 1648, she quickly formed the first African–European alliance against a European oppressor. Nzingha did not know at first that the Dutch were no different than the Portuguese with regard to colonization and slavery.

After a prolonged conflict with the Portuguese, Nzingha grew weary. The Portuguese were just as weary of her. Some historians suggest that she knew her various alliances were falling apart, and rather than negotiate from a position of weakness she once again negotiated a peace treaty with the Portuguese in 1656. It was, at best, an uneasy peace, because neither Nzingha nor the Portuguese trusted the other. Nzingha never retreated from her position against slavery until, according to Portuguese records, Nzingha died on December 17, 1663.

Her resistance to colonization and slavery as it was practiced by European powers spread far and wide. Her legacy has an American connection. The Portuguese name Angola comes from the term "king," or *ngola* or *n'gola*. It has been said that, during the eighteenth and nineteenth centuries, roughly seven out of every ten Africans imported into Charleston, South Carolina, came from the area called Angola near the Congo River. The language patterns of the people who occupy the Sea Islands off the coast of Georgia and South Carolina are very close to the structure of Kimbundu, a Bantu language, the same one spoken by Nzingha. Even the name the Sea Island slaves called themselves and their language, Gullah, is derived from Angola or most likely "ngola."

In South America, the Portuguese colony of Brazil received the largest number of Angolan captives. In modern-day Brazil, descendants of these slaves still hold ceremonies to celebrate Nzingha's resistance against slavery. Stories say that among the slaves it was believed that Nzingha sent warriors to Brazil to organize a resistance movement and plant the seeds of rebellion. There is some evidence of truth in the legend. As Nzingha fought in the hills of Angola, one of her kinsmen, a warrior named Zumbi, also known as Angola Janga — or Little Angola — escaped from a plantation and set up a colony for runaway slaves in northern Brazil.

Unfortunately, Angola remains a war-torn country, but

the spirit of Nzingha continues to speak to her people. As one biographer wrote in the sevententh century, "Because of her quest for freedom and relentless drive to bring peace to her people, Nzingha remains a glimmering symbol of inspiration."

(2) Kangela                    ==    Ngola Ndambi Kiluanji    ==    (1) [first wife,
(c. 1560s–c. 1616)                        (c. 1560–c. 1617)                name unknown]

Nzingha              Mukambu              Kifunji                Mbandi
(c. 1582–1663)      (c. 1584–c. 1670s)    (c. 1587–?)          (c. 1579–1623)

# The Kiluanji Family Tree

The Mbundu are the largest ethnic group, and one of the most ancient peoples, of the modern nation of Angola. They are divided into many kingdoms or subgroups, among them the Lenge, Songo, Mbondo, Hungu, Pende, Libolo, Ndongo, and Imbangala. Each group is made up of clans or lineages that are matrilineal, or descended from the mother. Among the Mbundu, each person is identified with their mother's clan, and all marriages of individuals are also marriages of clans.

Nzingha's mother was a captive slave. This meant that she had been removed completely from her clan or larger family and taken into another group. She had no relatives and could only be a *jaga*, an "outsider." Though Nzingha was First Daughter of the ruler, or Ngola, of Ndongo, she and her sisters were also considered "outsiders."

Mbundu history was preserved in ritual, art and craft, and in an oral tradition. Some versions of Mbundu oral history were written down in the 1600s. Despite these records, scholars' research, and interviews, large gaps still exist in our knowledge of events, and there is virtually no record of family relationships and personal histories. The family tree illustrates what we know of Nzingha's lineage. Names and dates of births and deaths are noted where available. The crown symbol indicates those who ruled. Double lines represent marriages; single lines indicate parentage.

**Ngola Ndambi Kiluanji:** The father of Queen Nzingha, he became Ngola during the Portuguese's first attempt to colonize the Ndongo territory. He married Kangela, even though the elders of the clans and his family protested their union. To satisfy his family, Kiluanji married an acceptable first wife, and Kangela became his secondary wife. He was thought to have been a strong opponent of the Portuguese.

**Kangela:** Mother of Nzingha and her two sisters, Mukambu and Kifunji. She died sometime after 1616.

## Children of Ngola Kiluanji

**Nzingha Ndambi:** Born around 1582, she was Ngola of Ndongo from 1624–1626, and queen of Matamba from 1630–1663. Nzingha was also known as Doña Ana de Sousa, the Christian name she took in Luanda. Nzingha was a strong, skillful Ndongo leader, building a mobile army that she herself led in battle against the Portuguese conquista. She had a special insight into the lives of captive slaves through her mother's (and her own) plight, and was deeply opposed to the type of slavery the Portuguese slave trade supported. In present-day Angola, Queen Nzingha is a cultural hero.

**Ngola Mbandi**: Son of Ngola Ndambi Kiluanji and his first wife. He showed no interest in becoming a chief, nor did he possess the skill to be one. Despite his weaknesses, he became Ngola in 1617 because he was the son of a Ngola and a proper mother. He died in 1623.

**Mukambu**: Loyal sister of Queen Nzingha. She took over the leadership of the Mbundu people in Matamba upon Nzingha's death in 1663.

**Kifunji**: Youngest sister of Queen Nzingha; she was born around 1587.

*Images of Nzingha are extremely rare. This sketch is of the oft–mentioned incident wherein Nzingha sat on the back of a servant to speak from an equal position with the Portuguese governor, who received her while seated.*

*A striking photograph of an African warrior from the Congo, circa 1910.*

*This young boy proudly shows off teeth filed to sharp points, a longtime practice of the Imbangala people.*

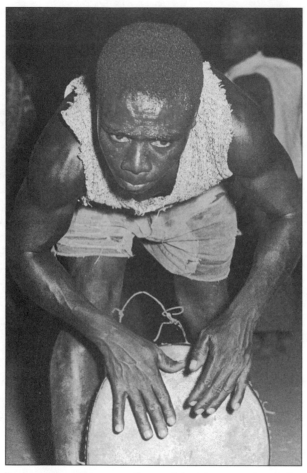

*The beating of drums is an integral part of the culture. Angolan artifacts often symbolize such common customs and rituals.*

*This wooden carving is symbolic of men beating drums to send messages, ward off evil spirits, or for tribal celebrations.*

*With practice, from a young age, women learn to transport items in this manner.*

*This carved wooden figure imitates the custom of women carrying baskets or bundles on their heads.*

*Portuguese settlers in Angola established* fazendas, *large commercial colonial farms, where they grew such crops as coffee, bananas, and sugarcane.*

*Luanda today. The capital of Angola, Luanda has grown into a bustling cosmopolitan city on the southwest Atlantic coast of Africa.*

*Thatched cottages of a village on the outskirts of Luanda illustrate the diversity in lifestyles from city to countryside. The church, introduced long ago by Portuguese missionaries, continues to be an integral part of the lives of Angolans.*

*In rural Angola, women engage in various means of commerce to earn income for their families. (top) Selling foods they have grown, sweet potatoes and yams, at roadside markets. (bottom) Crocheting lace for sale. (across) Pounding grain.*

115

*For Portuguese colonists in Angola in the sixteenth century, slave trading was major commerce. This engraving depicts a typical caravan of African captives traveling on the road, bound and shackled together.*

A SLAVE-SHED.

*This woodcut shows captives waiting in a common holding shed before being taken aboard the slave ship.*

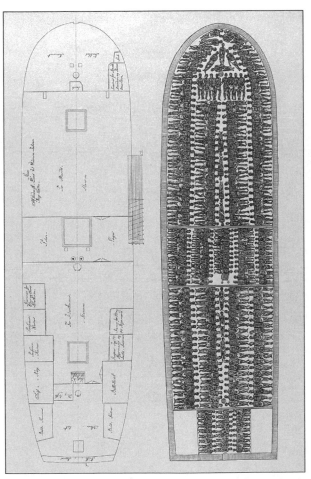

*A woodcut of the deck plan of a seventeenth-century slave ship. Aboard such a ship as this, slaves were packed tightly in the extremely close quarters, as shown, suffering all kinds of illnesses and death throughout the long, grueling journey at sea.*

*Slave ship bound for America. This drawing by Walter Appleton Clark illustrates Africans leaping overboard in a desperate attempt to escape their sad fate.*

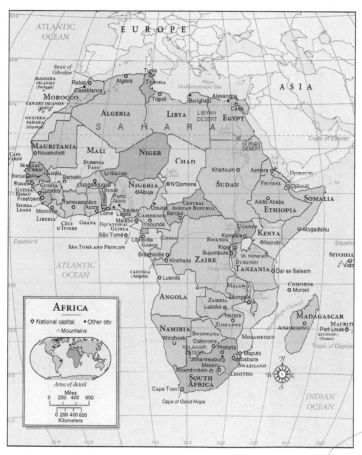

*Modern map of Africa. Angola is in the southwest region. The largest numbers of slaves from Angola were taken to the Portuguese colony of Brazil, South America. The inset map shows South America across from Africa, seperated by the Atlantic Ocean. The asterisk symbol indicates the location of Brazil, where today, descendants of slaves hold ceremonies to honor Nzingha.*

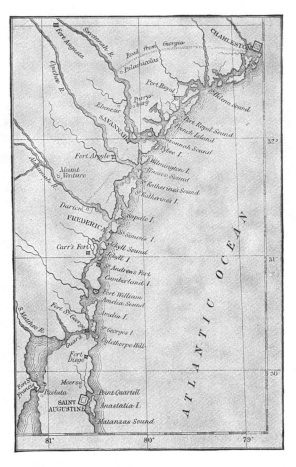

At the northeastern corner of the map is Charleston, South Carolina, and next to it, Georgia. Off the coast are the Sea Islands. A great number of slaves who were brought from Angola to the Americas ended up here. Their language and the name they called themselves, Gullah, comes from their native word "ngola."

*The Gullah people have not only maintained ancestral traditions and customs, but also trades such as weaving, seen today in the motherland. A Gullah woman* (top) *hand-weaving a sweetgrass basket for sale.* (bottom) *Similar baskets woven from reeds in Southern Angola.*

# Pronunciation Guide

### KIMBUNDU WORDS AND NAMES

* Indicates that the person/place/thing is fictionalized. All other names are based on real people and places in Mbundu history.

| | |
|---|---|
| *Ajala | ah-JAH-lah |
| *Azeze | ah-ZEH-zeh |
| Chokwe | CHOKE-weh |
| Imbangala | eem-BAHN-gah-lah |
| Jaga | JAH-gah |
| Kabasa | kah-BA-sah |
| Kafushe Kambare | kah-FOO-sheh kahm-BAH-reh |
| Kenjela | kehn-JAY-lah |
| Kifunji | kee-FOON-jee |
| Kiluanji | kee-loo-AHN-jee |
| Kimbundu | keem-BUN-doo |
| Kwanza | KWAHN-zah |
| *Kwumi | KWOO-mee |
| Luanda | loo-AHN-dah |
| Matamba | mah-TAHM-bah |
| Mbandi | MBAHN-dee |

| | |
|---|---|
| Mbangala | MBAHN-gah-lah |
| Mbundu | MBOON-doo |
| Mukambu | moo-KAHM-boo |
| Ndele | NDEH-leh |
| Ndongo | NDOHN-go |
| Ngola | NGOH-lah |
| *Ngulu | NGOO-loo |
| *Njali | NJAH-lee |
| Ntandi | NTAHN-dee |
| Nzingha | NZIN-gah (also seen as Nzinga) |
| *Pange | PAHNG |
| Zai | ZAH-ee |
| Zambu | ZAHM-boo |

## PORTUGUESE WORDS AND NAMES

| | |
|---|---|
| Abril | a-BREEL |
| Fevereiro | fe-ve-RAY-ru |
| Janeiro | jah-NAY-ru |
| Junho | JOO-nyoo |
| Março | MAHR-sso |
| Pombeiros | pom-BAY-ros |
| Quarta-feira | KWAR-tuh FAY-ruh |
| Quinta-feira | KEEN-tuh FAY-ruh |

| | |
|---|---|
| Domingo | do-MEEN-go |
| Setembro | se-TEM-bro |
| Terça-feira | TIR-suh FAY-ruh |
| | |
| Diogo Cão | DEE-o-go kow |
| Dom Jeronimo | don jir-OH-nee-mo |
| Dom João Furtado | don jo-OW foor-TAH-do de |
| de Mendonça | men-DON-sah |
| Fernando João | fer-NAN-do jo-OW kah-RAY- |
| Carreida de Sousa | da de SSOH-zah |
| Giovanni Gavazzi | zhee-oh-VAH-nee gah- |
| | VAHTS-ee |
| Paulo Dias de Novães | POW-loo DEE-az de no- |
| | VAYSH |
| São Domingo | sow do-MEEN-go |

# Glossary of Characters, Places & Things

**Abril** is the Portuguese word for April.

*__Ajala__ means "old woman." Older women were highly regarded among the Mbundu people.

*__Azeze__ is a fictional character. We know that Nzingha married and that her husband died in battle shortly after their son was born.

**Cão, Diogo** (Captain) was a Portuguese explorer.

**Chokwe** were a group of people who lived in eastern Angola. They were known for being traders and merchants.

**Domingo** is the Portuguese word for Sunday.

**Fevereiro** is the Portuguese word for February.

**Gavazzi, Giovanni** was a Portuguese priest who was a frequent visitor to Nzingha's father's court. He wrote a book about the Ngolas of Ndongo in the 1640s.

**Imbangala** were mercenary warriors who allied themselves with Nzingha after she became queen. After her death, the Imbangala became allies of the Portuguese and participated in the slave trade by raiding villages and selling the captives to the Portuguese.

**Jaga** means "outsiders." Since Nzingha took in any warrior who was willing to follow her command, she was often called the "Jaga Queen."

**Janeiro** is the Portuguese word for January.

**Jeronimo, Dom** was once the Governor of Luanda.

**Kabasa** is the capital city of the Mbundu people.

**Kafushe Kambare** was an Imbangala leader who allied with Kiluanji against the Portuguese.

**Kenjela** was the mother of Nzingha and her sisters. She was a slave who became a wife of the Ngola.

**Kifunji** was the youngest sister of Nzingha. She was captured and held by the Portuguese for six years. She was killed in battle.

**Kiluanji** was Nzingha's father and Ngola of the Mbundu people.

**Kimbundu** was the language spoken by the Mbundu.

**Kwanza** is a river in Angola near the capital of Mbundu.

*__Kwumi__ is a fictional character, the mother of Mbandi.

**Luanda** is the capital city of present-day Angola. It was the first Portuguese settlement in Angola.

**Março** is the Portuguese word for March.

**Matamba** is the kingdom that Nzingha forged out of runaway slaves, mercenary soldiers, and loyal members of the Mbundu army. Although Nzingha's homeland was Ndongo, she never ruled there.

**Mbandi** was the half-brother of Nzingha. He had Nzingha's son murdered and later went mad. Because of his poor leadership, the Portuguese invaded Ndongo and burned Kabasa. The Portuguese chose a puppet Ngola to rule Ndongo.

**Mbangala** is the dry season between July and November.

**Mbundu** were a large group of Angolan people who occupied the northwestern part of Angola known as Ndongo.

**Mendonça, Dom João Furtado de** was once the Governor of Luanda.

**Mukambu** was the second sister of Nzingha. She converted to Christianity and ruled Matamba after Nzingha.

**Ndele** means "white-winged bird."

**Ndongo** was the homeland of the Mbundu people before the Portuguese invasion. Nzingha led her people eastward into the mountains where she established Matamba, the new home for the Mbundu who followed her.

**Ngola** is the term used for a Mbundu leader.

*__Ngulu__ means "pig." Neither Nzingha nor her sisters had a parrot by this name. However, parrots were favorite pets of royalty.

*__Njali__ is a fictional character, a member of the Imbangala people. According to historical notes, Nzingha made friends with Imbangala soldiers who fought for her father. It is even suggested that she might have married one of them. There is no record of her first husband, other than that they were both very young.

**Nováes, Paulo Dias de** was held as a hostage by Nzingha's grandfather from 1561–1565. He recommended sending troops to Ndongo to defeat the Mbundu. He served as the first governor of Luanda.

*__Ntandi__ is a fictional character.

**Nzingha** (also seen as **Nzinga**) was probably one of the most interesting and colorful female leaders in world history. Unlike many of her contemporaries, she was not only a leader, but a general as well. She fought alongside her soldiers.

*Pange means "brother."

Pombeiros means "Afro-Portuguese."

Presidio means "fort."

Quarta-feira is the Portuguese word for Wednesday.

Quinta-feira is the Portuguese word for Thursday.

Setembro is the Portuguese word for September.

Sousa, Fernando João Carreida de was once the Governor of Luanda.

*Susanna is a fictional character.

Terça-feira is the Portuguese word for Tuesday.

Zai means "knowledge."

Zambu are trees that grow so close together, a person could swing from tree to tree without having to touch the ground.

# About the Author

Patricia C. McKissack first learned about Nzingha of Angola from a promotional poster entitled "Great Kings and Queens of Africa," produced by Anheuser Busch Brewery, Inc. Although the biographical note that accompanied the portrait was limited, it was enough to inspire McKissack to find out more about the warrior-diplomat who for decades held Portuguese invaders in check.

"Researching the life of Nzingha was a learning experience for me. I had never heard of this remarkable woman, but I am proud to know about Nzingha now. Her story is well worth telling," says the author, whose research for this project took some unusual twists and turns. "For example," McKissack continues, "while in Lisbon, Portugal, during the fall of 1999, my husband, Fredrick [co-author of a number of my books] and I visited maritime and military museums in search of information about Angola's military queen. Unfortunately, we didn't find very much about her there. Then, purely by accident, we stumbled upon a tiny bookstore where we found an old biography of Nzingha. I paid four dollars for it, but to me, it was a treasure — a rare and wonderful find — even though it was written in Portuguese."

With the help of the Internet and the Washington University inter-library loan system, McKissack discovered that the book was originally published by a British company, but the book was no longer in print. Still, within two weeks she was able to find and borrow the English edition from the University of Virginia. "We live in the golden age of information," says McKissack. "It's a great time for writers."

Born in a small town outside Nashville, Tennessee, Pat McKissack attended Tennessee State University where she majored in English. "I've always loved history — especially African and African-American history. Wanting to know more about my own culture and wanting to share that knowledge with others is the motivation that keeps me writing."

Although McKissack has written over one hundred books for young readers of all ages, this is her first book in

The Royal Diaries series. Two McKissack books are in the Dear America series: *A Picture of Freedom: The Diary of Clotee, a Slave Girl, 1859* and *Color Me Dark: The Diary of Nellie Lee Love, Chicago, 1919.* Both have been made into successful HBO specials. McKissack is also the award-winning author of *Mirandy and Brother Wind, Flossie and the Fox, It's the Honest-to-Goodness Truth,* and *The Dark Thirty: Southern Tales of the Supernatural,* a Newbery Honor Book. Books co-authored with her husband, Fredrick, include *Christmas in the Big House; Christmas in the Quarters,* a Coretta Scott King Award for text, *Ain't I a Woman? The Biography of Sojourner Truth,* a Boston Globe/Horn Book Award, and *Let My People Go, Old Testament Bible Stories,* which received an NAACP Image Award for Children's Books, 1999. Their most recent Scholastic title is *Black Hands, White Sails,* a Coretta Scott King Honor book for text, 2000.

The McKissacks, who have been married since 1964, are the parents of three adult sons who live with their families in St. Louis, Missouri and Memphis, Tennessee. The McKissacks live and work in Chesterfield, Missouri, where they enjoy tending a patio garden, bargain hunting for antiques, and watching old and new movies. When they aren't traveling for research, they travel for fun.

# Acknowledgments

Cover painting by Tim O'Brien

Page 105: Nzingha seated on servant, Tim O'Brien.
Page 106: Warrior from Congo, Hulton Getty Picture Library,
    Laure Communications, New York, New York.
Page 107: Boy with filed teeth, Laure Communications, New York,
    New York.
Page 108: Drummer, Black Star, New York, New York.
Page 109: Carved drummer, Paula and Ruth Tishman Collection, M&E
    Bernheim, Woodfin Camp & Associates, New York, New York.
Page 110: Woman with bundle, Giacomo Pirozzi, Panos Pictures,
    London, England.
Page 111: Carved woman with basket, M&E Bernheim, Woodfin Camp &
    Associates, New York, New York.
Page 112 (top): Portuguese farm, Laure Communications, New York,
    New York.
Page 112 (bottom): Portuguese farmers, Laure Communications,
    New York, New York.
Page 113 (top): Cosmopolitan Luanda, Volkmar Wentzel,
    National Geographic Image Collection.

Page 113 (bottom): Village outside Luanda, Volkmar Wentzel, National Geographic Image Collection.

Page 114 (top): Women at roadside market, Giacomo Pirozzi, Panos Pictures, London, England.

Page 114 (bottom): Women crocheting, Giacomo Pirozzi, Panos Pictures, London, England.

Page 115: Women pounding grain, Giacomo Pirozzi, Panos Pictures, London, England.

Page 116 (top): Slave caravan, North Wind Picture Archives, Alfred, Maine.

Page 116 (bottom): Slaves in holding shed, North Wind Picture Archives, Alfred, Maine.

Page 117: Deck plan of slave ship, North Wind Picture Archives, Alfred, Maine.

Page 118: Africans leaping overboard ship, North Wind Picture Archives, Alfred, Maine.

Page 119: Map of Africa, Jim McMahon.

Page 120: Map of South Carolina, North Wind Picture Archives, Alfred, Maine.

Page 121 (top): Woman weaving basket, Gerard Fritz, TRANSPARENCIES Inc.

Page 121 (bottom): Woven baskets, Jason Laure, Laure Communications, New York, New York.

To Onawumi Jean Moss

# Other books in The Royal Diaries series

ELIZABETH I
Red Rose of the House of Tudor
*by Kathryn Lasky*

CLEOPATRA VII
Daughter of the Nile
*by Kristiana Gregory*

MARIE ANTOINETTE
Princess of Versailles
*by Kathryn Lasky*

ISABEL
Jewel of Castilla
*by Carolyn Meyer*

ANASTASIA
The Last Grand Duchess
*by Carolyn Meyer*

Copyright © 2000 by Patricia C. McKissack.

■ ▤ ■

All rights reserved. Published by Scholastic Inc.
555 Broadway, New York, NY 10012.
SCHOLASTIC, THE ROYAL DIARIES, and associated logos are trademarks and/or registered trademarks of Scholastic Inc.

Library of Congress Cataloging-in-Publication Data
McKissack, Pat, 1944–
Nzingha, warrior queen of Matamba / by Patricia C. McKissack.
p. cm. – (The royal diaries)
Summary: Presents the diary of thirteen-year-old Nzingha, a sixteenth-century West African princess who loves to hunt and hopes to lead her kingdom one day against the invasion of the Portuguese slave traders.
ISBN 0-439-11210-9
1. Nzingha, Queen of Matamba, d. 1663—Juvenile fiction. 2. Angola—History—1482–1648—Juvenile fiction. [1. Nzingha, Queen of Matamba, d.1663—Fiction. 2. Angola—History—1482–1648—Fiction. 3. Princesses—Fiction. 4. Blacks—Angola—Fiction. 5. Mbundu (African people)—Fiction. 6. Slave trade—Fiction. 7. Sex role—Fiction. 8. Diaries—Fiction.] I. Title. II. Series.
PZ7.M478693 Nz 2000
[Fic]—dc21                                                                                  00-024216

12  11  10  9                                                                              04

The display type was set in Augereau.
The text type was set in Cutamond Basic.
Book design by Elizabeth B. Parisi

Printed in the U.S.A.    23
First printing, September 2000

■ ▤ ■